Scary Old Sex

STORIES

ARLENE HEYMAN

BLOOMSBURY

NEW YORK · LONDON · OXFORD · NEW DELHI · SYDNEY

Bloomsbury USA
An imprint of Bloomsbury Publishing Plc

1385 Broadway	50 Bedford Square
New York	London
NY 10018	WC1B 3DP
USA	UK

www.bloomsbury.com

Versions of these stories previously appeared in the following publications: "Artifact" in the magazine *Epoch*, and "In Love with Murray" in the Japanese translation by Nobuko Katsui of *Bernard Malamud: A Writer's Life* by Philip Davis. "Dancing" originally appeared in *Epoch* magazine. A version of "Night Call" first appeared in *Podium*, an online literary magazine of the Unterberg Poetry Center at New York's 92nd Street Y, 2009.

"Rose-Marie," lyrics by Otto Harbach and Oscar Hammerstein II; music by Rudolf Friml and Herbert Stothart. Copyright ©1925, Renewed 1953. Bill/Bob Publishing Company/ ASCAP/Bambalina Music Publishing Company/ASCAP/Warner Brothers, Inc./ASCAP. Copyright © 1924 Williamson Music (ASCAP), Warner/Chappell Music, Inc. and Songwriters Guild of America. Copyright © 1924, 1925 (Copyrights Renewed) WB Music Corp., Bambalina Music and Bill/Bob Publishing Co. All rights reserved. Used by permission.

ISBN:	HB:	978-1-63286-233-4
	ePub:	978-1-63286-235-8

LIBRARY OF CONGRESS CATALOGING-IN-PUBLICATION DATA

Heyman, Arlene.
[Short stories. Selections]
Scary old sex : stories / Arlene Heyman.
pages cm
ISBN 978-1-63286-233-4
I. Title.
PS3608.E927A6 2015
813'.6—dc23
2015012211

2 4 6 8 10 9 7 5 3 1

Typeset by RefineCatch Limited, Bungay, Suffolk
Printed and bound in USA by Berryville Graphics Inc., Berryville, Virginia

For Len, and in memory of Shepard

CONTENTS

THE LOVES OF HER LIFE

"WOULD YOU LIKE to make love?" Stu called out to Marianne as she entered their apartment. She walked toward his office. It was mid-Saturday afternoon and Stu was still in his purple pajamas at the computer, a mug of coffee on the cluttered desk. He had a little wet mocha-colored stain under his lip on his beard, and his wiry gray hair stood up thinly around his large bald spot. He looked at her shyly for a moment, then looked back at the computer screen. His office was a small room off the entrance foyer, the glossy hardwood floor littered with unruly piles of papers and journals—she spotted *Dissent*, *MIT Technology Review*, the *Hightower Lowdown*. Beside these were stuffed canvas bags, a white one imprinted with SCHLEPPEN in black, a bright-blue one with multicolored flowers above the words GREENPEACE RAINBOW WARRIOR. Unframed photos of children and grandchildren lay scattered on the marble radiator cover.

Marianne had just come back from a frenetic brunch with her son, Billy, at a bistro on Madison Avenue and hadn't yet taken off her coat. Because his wife was divorcing him, Billy was distraught. From her point of view as an ex-social worker, Marianne had always considered her son's wife a borderline personality—from the human point of view, an outright bitch. And Marianne would have rejoiced that they were divorcing except that Billy was distraught. She had tried to comfort him at the same time that she was urging him not to give in to his wife's outrageous demands: Lyria wanted the apartment and the country house and half of Billy's business. "Only half?" Marianne had asked, but Billy was deaf to her sarcasm. He put away one Grey Goose after another while the poached eggs he'd ordered turned into hard yellow eyes and he kept making throat-clearing, half-gagging sounds, sounds he'd made occasionally when he got anxious as a kid; she didn't think she'd heard those sounds in twenty-five years. She had joined him in a Grey Goose herself, trying to smooth away her edginess, and since she rarely drank, she was still tipsy. Marianne wanted either to go to the gym to work it off or try for a drop-in appointment at her hairdresser's where she would be cosseted. She could use some cosseting.

But she knew how hard it was for her husband to ask for sex, even after three wives; Marianne was his fourth. Why was it so hard? The best Stu had come up with was fear of rejection. She didn't understand—if you were out one day, you might be in the next. But he was reluctant even to ask for all dark meat from the Chirping Chicken take-out place and also he tended to buy the first item a salesperson showed him. His timidity annoyed her. He thought he was just an easygoing, nice guy. Cooperative. And many agreed with him.

She had other resentments, some small. He never brought her flowers, although she adored flowers. "I buy you printer cartridges," he'd said. "And flash drives."

Some resentments were chasm sized. He didn't make enough money, and what he made he was always giving to obscure political groups working for "social justice" or to one of his numerous importuning adult children—the major beneficiaries of his modest will.

And he dressed badly, and called her superficial when she complained, though lately he had let her go clothes shopping with him. Clothes delighted her. A tall, slender woman with prominent cheekbones, slanted blue eyes, and dramatic silver-white hair, Marianne attracted admiration—she did a little modeling for Eileen Fisher, one of the few fashion designers whose ads occasionally featured older women. She was proud of being, hands down, the best-looking of his wives. He loved her, she knew, in part for her looks, and so it wasn't fair that he criticized her for caring how *he* looked.

And couldn't he be even a little seductive, instead of asking for sex as if he were asking for a game of tennis?

In spite of it all, or perhaps because of it, she tried never to reject him when he asked: it softened her up toward him, making love. And it got him away from his computer, and connected him to another human being—namely, her. She tried to do it at least once a week.

It didn't sound like much: she had made love three or four times a week with her first husband, who'd been younger than she, and who had died eleven years ago. But now that she was sixty-five and Stu seventy, spontaneity was difficult. She had acid reflux, and so had to stay upright for two or three hours after a meal or else suffer burning pains in her chest. And she had to insert Vagifem, low-level estrogen tablets, in her vagina twice a week so her tissues didn't thin out. He used Viagra half an hour before sex, and because he tended to come too soon if they weren't making love often, and once a week wasn't often, he also took a dose of clomipramine, an antidepressant that had as a side effect retarded ejaculation. The Viagra made him feel flushed for the rest of the day and the clomipramine made him spacey. So they usually had sex toward evening, if not at night.

He didn't really come too soon; he never came until after she climaxed. But she got most of her pleasure from inter-course *after* she had come, an oddity, perhaps, but that was how she was. She hated remembering what sex had been like for her in her twenties, before she'd accepted herself, and when the received wisdom was that you weren't a real woman unless you came vaginally—that is, no hands. The huffing and puffing and the squeals and screams of orgasmic pleasure she had faked! And this was in the dawning age of feminism! She had heard from a neighbor, a high school teacher, that even now freshman girls were sucking off senior boys without getting anything in return.

While Stu wanted to last after she had come, it was difficult. If she told him, as he was thrusting after her orgasm, "God, this feels good," he immediately came. If she said nothing, merely looked beatific, he also came. So now, ironically, she suppressed any noises she might have made and often lied to him that she *hadn't* come in order to keep him at it. And if he got notice that she wanted to make love, he masturbated ten hours before, because then he definitely lasted longer. In short, for them, making love was like running a war: plans had to be drawn up, equipment in tiptop condition, troops deployed and coordinated meticulously, there was no room for maverick actions lest the country end up defeated and at each other's throats . . .

So she called to him now, "Yes, dear, that would be very nice, making love." She removed from her pocketbook the note card on which she always wrote down the time she had taken her last bite of any meal, checked her watch, and did the acid reflux calculation: "Give me forty-five minutes, please." She hung up her coat, leaned against the wall for a moment to steady herself from the alcohol, while she watched him hotfoot it out of his office to the bathroom medicine chest, where he took his pills. He joined her in the foyer, gave her a little hug. Then he returned to his computer to keep working until the medicine would take effect.

"No frills today, huh?" she called after him, disappointed that he'd gone back to work. They might have talked about Billy's predicament, or this or that.

"The server's down in New Jersey and I've got a hundred e-mail complaints." His eyes were fixed on the screen.

She walked down the long hallway to their black-and-white-painted bedroom and undressed there, put on a loose cotton robe. Placing some pillows between her back and the wall, she sat down in the lotus position on the kilim and did some breathing exercises, then tried to meditate. Her son's wretchedness kept intruding itself; she had images of slapping Lyria around until her face was the same color as her long, flaming hair, Lyria who didn't work or cook or clean, who took voice lessons but never sang when anyone was around to hear. A silent, sullen diva. She would pout or suddenly go into a tirade at Billy, no matter who was around to hear. Their apartment, littered with musical scores and smelling of cat piss—she owned half a dozen Persian cats, which she didn't take care of, so the place was covered with hair—was uninhabitable. Marianne and her first

husband, and now just Marianne, had paid for years of therapy
for Lyria, without so much as a thank-you. Or any sign of improvement. Yet Billy loved this woman. Although Marianne
repeated and repeated her mantra, she could not block out her
daughter-in-law's high, thin voice. Finally Marianne gave up.
She showered, put on a sleek sky-blue nightgown, swirled a
minty mouthwash around in her mouth to get rid of the taste
of vodka.

She and Stu used to watch porn sometimes to warm up
for sex, but not after she'd read Gloria Steinem's essay about
how Linda Lovelace was beaten and literally enslaved by her
husband and keeper, Chuck Traynor; after Lovelace managed
to escape, the same man married Marilyn Chambers and
treated her the same way. With that knowledge, watching
Deep Throat or *Behind the Green Door* was worse than crossing
a picket line. So she resorted to her own manifold fantasies.
She had asked him did he fantasize while making love and he
said no, he thought about her. He didn't ask about her. Was this
an unliberated aspect of their marriage, that they didn't tell
each other their fantasies? He claimed he didn't have mastur-
batory fantasies. What he had was an "athletic sex" video on his
computer: he did everything at his computer.

Now she got into bed under the bright-white duvet and
readied the box of tissues and the tube of K-Y Jelly.

He came in naked and she remembered again why she did
not like to make love in the daytime. She joked sometimes
that no one over forty should be allowed to make love in the
daytime. There he was, every wrinkle exposed, as if he were in
a Lucian Freud painting. He had loose flesh on his chest, small
sagging breasts beneath his nipples, and little pink outgrowths

here and there. His pubic hair was colorless and sparse, and he happened to have the smallest penis she had ever seen, although he was a large bear of a man. His penis looked like a small round neck with an eyeless face barely peeking out above his pouchlike scrotum. When she got angry at him, she felt like telling him so, yelling it out, but she figured if she did that, he'd never get another erection; and erect, he was big enough to do the job so long as they didn't use Astroglide or any of those thin liquid lubricants. She couldn't feel him then. But the thick K-Y Jelly provided some traction and he did just fine.

She didn't like how *she* looked anymore, either. Her breasts and waist were not bad, maybe better than that, if you ignored the yearning her breasts seemed to have developed for her waist. But tiny, bright-red raised spots had appeared here and there on her torso—she recalled her father had had them in old age. And her ass and thighs were bony, the flesh hanging a little. And while her pubic hair was still blondish brown, you could see the skin beneath. Where was that thick bush of yesteryear?

He moved in next to her under the duvet. It was winter and, mercifully, the whole episode might take place under cover. Although once she got into it, she got into it, and also she kept her eyes and her critical faculties shut, at least mostly.

She moved into a spoon position with her back up against his chest and her ass against his penis. She felt him grow hard. He tried to turn her toward him and she resisted for a moment, then yielded. "Talk to me," she said. "Tell me something intimate."

He laughed. "You first."

She said, "I'm afraid I'll die without ever making another movie I'm proud of." After being a social worker for years, in

an act of bravery or foolishness, she had trained as a docu-
mentary filmmaker. But she had trouble raising money—her
first husband had underwritten her two best films—and since
he died, she'd shot mostly commercials.

Stu said, "I have three faculty members coming up for tenure
and I have to read their books. And I've put it off and off."

"That's not intimate. That's something you'd tell anyone.
Tell me something you'd tell only me, your wife."

"You want me to share some misery with you. I don't have
any. I'm a contented man. I love my work." He paused. "And
I love my wife."

She kissed him hard.

He began rubbing her nipples.

"Not like that, sweetie. You're doing it mechanically. Pull
on them. Bite them a little. Pay some concentrated attention."

He obliged. She lay back and after a moment felt the sensa-
tions start high up, way back in her vagina. Higher. What was
higher than that? The cervix, the uterus—her first husband,
a doctor, had drawn her diagrams she vaguely remembered.
The cunt.

Too soon he said, "Shall I eat you?"

"Not yet. Don't stop doing what you're doing."

"I can do both at the same time."

"Always multitasking, aren't you."

He grinned and took a pillow from the bed and laid it on
the floor, then went down on his knees on the pillow and
she moved to the edge of the bed and opened her legs wide.
She ran her hands through his hair that was still sticking up. He
needed a haircut. He often needed a haircut and a beard trim—
he let white stubble grow on his cheeks sometimes for days,

and on his neck; he just didn't notice. Evidently nobody else noticed, either, at least no one commented to him about it, but it offended her aesthetic sensibilities. And in bed it scratched her face, and occasionally the skin on the inside of her thighs. She would sometimes shave him herself, although she wasn't into cutting his hair. Now he opened the tube of K-Y Jelly and smeared some on her nipples, then pulled at them while he ran his tongue over her clitoris. She found herself thinking about her strawberry-blond-haired granddaughter, Jeanine, age four, who had smeared bright-orange finger paints all over her legs and face, laughing delightedly. She had smeared them on her grandma as well, and they ended up taking a bubble bath together in the master bathroom. Would it be more difficult to see her granddaughter, now that her son was getting divorced? Not if Billy got joint custody or at least decent visiting rights— he might even bring Jeanine around *more*, for what was a single man to do by himself with a small child? Well, she supposed these were unliberated thoughts as well, for there were many men now who helped bring up the children. Her deceased husband, David, had been pretty good with Billy, even sewing up rips in his clothes, although David had been the busiest of orthopedic surgeons. How witty and playful he was, once paint-ing flowers on her ass in bed; another time he had constructed a man with a fuse box for a chest and a papier-mâché face and put pajamas on him and had the creature waiting under the covers for her when she came in expecting to make love. Now she thought she couldn't let herself think about David. She'd get sad and wonder why she had to be with Stu instead of with David, why did David have to have a heart attack at fifty-two and die? Lean and light-boned David, who'd run six marathons, pale skin shiny with suntan lotion, bush of black hair sweat-slicked to his scalp. She could still see him in his signature red shorts and black T-shirt reaching out to take the paper cup of water someone offered him, barely breaking his stride.

Death had come out of nowhere. David was playing a fathers-and-grown-up-sons ball game with Billy, Billy who had the same fair, eager-to-burn skin, the same perspicacious hazel eyes. David had run after a long ball in that effortless, loose-limbed, almost jaunty style of his, he'd leaped high, reached and got his glove on the ball, held on to it, held on to it, and collapsed. She had been sitting there watching, thought he was fooling around, she'd even stood up and applauded. Marianne knew if she pursued this line of thought she'd never come, and it wasn't fair to Stu, who was working away with his tongue. She bent over, blinking back tears, and kissed his head, then rubbed his neck for a while, massaged it. "Do you want to come in me, dear?"

He bobbed his head once but went on eating her. She put her hands under his armpits, trying to pull him up, and said, "It's enough, dear. I don't want you hurting yourself." He had arthritis in his neck, and once, while eating her, had developed back spasm and was laid up for a month—she'd waited on him hand and foot, sucked him off, and still felt guilty.

He got into bed beside her now and ran his tongue over her hand.

"Got a hair stuck in your mouth?" she asked him.

"Yes, but I'll swallow it."

"You don't have to. Wash your mouth out, honey. I can wait."

But he shook his head.

She took the tube of K-Y Jelly and squeezed some onto her fingers and lathered his penis with it, rubbing him to grow his erection. Slowly he entered her, and she put some jelly on her forefinger and started rubbing her clitoris while he moved in and out. He was over her, supporting himself on his hands, and she looked at his shaggy beard and knobby skin, which hung a little around his kindly face. She had cherished his kindness, remembered their first date at the Moroccan restaurant he'd taken her to, where the tablecloths were rose and chartreuse with little mirrors sewn on them. Did she eat? Through much of the meal she'd wept about her husband, dead a year, worried to this stranger that she was leeching the marrow out of her twenty-seven-year-old son whom she called sometimes two or three times a day to hear his scratchy-edgy voice, so like his father's. And Billy had his father's long, thin fingers—she'd made a short video of the movements of her son's hands. Billy'd quipped while she shot it that he didn't think the film would have wide appeal. And she bemoaned not having had more children with her husband. A daughter. And Stu listened and nodded and patted her arm, and passed her a little cellophane pack of tissues he carried with him because his nose was often congested.

Stu had seemed a little—oh, more than a little—heroic to her. His sheer size in the tiny restaurant. Big blocklike hands. They had their appeal. Still did. And some things he'd done back in the day impressed her, though she'd had to pull them out of him: he'd dreamed up software, armor really, that protected computer networks from attack—saved the traffic lights—imagine New York City without traffic lights! And one time he'd even gone in to rescue the police department from a hacker, although he had mixed feelings about police departments.

She closed her eyes now and kissed Stu with her tongue and opened her legs wide and, rubbing herself with one hand and caressing his neck with the other, imagined herself a stupid little girl, maybe twelve years old, who came to clean at a house of old men, one of whom explained to her that she'd get much smarter in school if she sucked semen out of them, that semen was the source of intelligence, and the more orifices of hers she could get their semen into, the smarter she'd be. And one man took her clothes off and began rubbing her little clitoris, and another put his old gray penis in her mouth and she sucked and sucked eagerly until she got some semen out of it and then she begged for more and sucked off another old man. Her job was to clean the house and they set her doing it in a servant's frock with no underpants on, so any old man who wanted could begin massaging her clitoris, and she would beg to suck him off. She didn't notice any improvement in her grades at school, but felt she had only just started with this sucking business and there were all her other openings and she wondered about her ears.

Stu continued moving in and out of her. Marianne nibbled at his neck and at his ears. She put more K-Y Jelly on her finger and imagined herself a woman in her twenties, with a shaved head and pussy, lying naked in a doorway while one woman rubbed her clitoris, another pulled at her nipples. There was a party going on inside and any man who was entering the party had to step over her. He was allowed to do anything he wanted to her, so long as he didn't hurt her. The women kept her in a constant state of excitement. A stranger might enter her casually while chatting with one of the women. Or he might chat with his friend who was accompanying him; the two might together enter Marianne, one in her mouth, one in her ass. One or the other might come on Marianne's belly and rub his semen all over her breasts.

Marianne kept rubbing herself, her husband kept thrusting, she felt she was almost there, almost there. She put more jelly on her finger and imagined herself a thirty-year-old woman on a stage making love with a younger man while an audience of Japanese businessmen took photos of her, one or another running up onstage to get a better shot. Occasionally the man who was banging her asked if anyone in the audience wanted to take over. Several rushed onto the stage. Soon there was a line snaking out the door.

In bed Marianne opened her legs as wide as she could, as if someone were forcing her open, and whispered urgently to Stu, "Stop moving! Stop!" She was starting to come, little waves of contractions passed through her, and if he kept moving, she would miss feeling them. She kept rubbing herself through the contractions, which intensified them, and finally when they stopped, she put her arms around Stu's back and kissed him deeply. After a moment, she said "Now." And he began to move gently, quietly, then forcefully in and out. And she tried very hard not to look pleased—she kept a frown on her face. She wanted to say, "Pull out if you feel you're going to come," but she was afraid to say anything.

She kept her eyes closed and he said, "Can I come now?"

"No!" she nearly hollered. He stopped moving, and they waited. Then he started again. "Tell me when I can come."

"Not yet."

Then his breathing got heavy, heavier. "I'm going to come," he said desperately, and then he was breathing heavily into her ear and made a few quick thrusts and fell onto her.

She had wanted more, and she felt disappointed, a little empty. Still, she kissed his face and he came out of her, put tissues on his penis and between her legs, and she got out of bed and hobbled to the bathroom holding the tissues in place, then dropped them into the toilet and peed. She washed her hands and breasts and washed between her legs and got back into bed. He was lying naked with tissues on his limp penis. She kissed him and spooned up against him. She thought to ask him, "Why couldn't you have held on just a little bit longer?" But he was already snoring, which was just as well. She'd complained to him a few times about his failure to last longer, but she never said why didn't he last as long as David had or why didn't he make even half the money David made. She did ask why couldn't he go with her to see an occasional avant-garde film, and wear a suit and tie on the rare occasions they went together to her arts club—she was chairperson of the film committee. And he'd yelled at her, "I give talks all over, and I'm treated with respect, like a valued person. Only at home am I sniped at."

He had slept on the living room couch that time—it was not the first time—and in the middle of the night, she'd gone in and apologized, and dragged his offended hulking self back into bed with her. She tried to get him to make love to her, but he wouldn't. "I'm not in a loving mood."

"It'll put you in a loving mood."

But he wouldn't.

Cleaning out their storage cages in the basement of the apartment building, she came upon boxes of documentation David had saved for income taxes. Stu said they could all be thrown out, they were more than ten years old, but she couldn't bear to throw away anything to do with her dead husband without at least looking over each item, including canceled checks (they reminded her of where they'd been and what they'd done). So she laid a tarp over the Oriental rug in the foyer, and Stu helped drag up the dusty boxes, some of which had dried bits of plaster in them; she vacuumed the boxes.

There were income tax returns that showed her husband had made half a million dollars some years, a million others, and that was when money was worth more. There were airline tickets and stamped documents proving that he had attended surgical conventions, which made their family trips tax-deductible. There were journals in which he'd published papers—he was an expert on repairing the labrum, a membrane in the hip joint, which often tore in athletes. In fact, he had invented the procedure. Other surgeons simply removed the damaged labrum, but sewing it up seemed to make for less arthritis in later life—at least that was the case in animal studies. The data were only now, decades later, starting to come in on humans, and a colleague of his told her everything seemed to bear her husband out. David would have been thrilled.

There were receipts from different restaurants where they'd eaten in Venice: Locanda Cipriani, Crepizza, il Cenacolo, da Bepi. She remembered the family watching a glassblower in Murano. From one of the thunderous red furnaces, the skinny, pockmarked fellow had pulled out a long pipe with reddish-yellow molten glass at the end of it. He'd blown into the pipe and the blob of glass expanded and elongated, and Billy, age seven, watched fiercely, swaying a little in the hot, noisy room, clasping and unclasping his hands. Marianne asked did he need to go to the bathroom, but the boy shook his head without taking his eyes off the changing glass. David hoisted Billy up onto his shoulders, where he sat rapt as the worker rolled the glass in dark-green powder and thrust it back into the furnace, blew it up again, and tweezed it, astonishingly, into the shape of a man playing the piano—all very small, but you could see the pianist's fingers and the piano keys. Billy bounced with delight on David's shoulders and begged to stay for another demonstration. Afterwards they ordered a whole orchestra of the small green-glass figurines for Billy, who was learning to play the trumpet at school. Billy now owned a bookstore, and he had those figurines out on a table in the books-on-music section. It was amazing that the orchestra had survived his childhood, so many years ago, intact. But Billy had been a careful, thoughtful boy. How had he married such a flailing, chaotic woman?

She remembered a shop on the Rio Terrà Canal, off Campo Santa Margherita, a shop that made masks; they'd bought the plague doctor for David, a papier-mâché face in black and white with small round glasses and a huge curved beak of a nose. (Anti-Semitic? No. In the Middle Ages a plague doctor wore a cone-shaped beak stuffed with herbs and straw to ward off "plague air.") She shook the dust off the mask onto the tarp.

Hadn't warded off anything.

Ever.

She remembered going to empty out David's office at the hospital, after he had died so suddenly. She had cried in the street and put the mask on momentarily to cover her tears. A little white boy holding an older black woman's hand had pointed at Marianne, reached up, and tried to touch the mask; he'd called out "trick or treat," though it was April.

She wanted to touch David, not the decayed David who was in that box; probably the bacteria had eaten away everything but the bones. Maybe the bones, those slim bones, were gone, too, by now.

She touched a receipt from a hotel in Spain, in Toledo. It was dated almost seven years earlier than the Venice receipts—she'd been pregnant with Billy. On a clear afternoon during the Easter season, they'd driven a rented car to Toledo. From a distance they could see most of the hilly, terraced town with its stone gray wall and the blue Tagus River winding round; Toledo looked so much like an El Greco painting that she half expected to see elongated figures in glowing robes walking the streets. She'd learned that the artist had lost commissions because of his hauteur and pomposity. Not to compare herself, but she'd been turned away by donors for understating what she could do as a filmmaker. She'd always had self-doubts.

Church bells rang throughout the day in different pitches and timbres. On the ancient walls, paper pictures of saints were taped, and red-and-white streamers flew overhead. Half the town seemed to consist of tourist shops. At dusk, the couple joined a solemn parade that was moving ponderously up to the *Catedral,* the great church of Toledo. Incense suffused the air. At the front of the line, in a gray robe, a monk carried a big wooden cross with a life-sized carved Jesus hanging from it. Marianne and David left before the procession reached its destination—they had seen so many churches that they felt weighted down by them—and made their way at first gravely, then giggling, two escapees, to their hotel. They ate—she remembered a rabbit-and-vegetable paella—in their penthouse suite, from which they could see the city lights glimmering in the night. Two big bottles of sparkling water, which tasted like champagne to them, accompanied the meal. David had joined her in abstinence; he claimed that not drinking and doing Lamaze with her brought him as close as he could get to the experience of being pregnant himself. Not drinking was actually easier for him than for her: she liked her glass of wine with dinner, but alcohol put him to sleep. They kept nonalcoholic beer in the refrigerator at home.

After dinner they undressed, Marianne keeping on only a heavy string of black pearls David had bought her on a trip to China. She'd had a head of thick blond hair back then; "my lioness," he'd teased her. He took a photo of her standing against the bay of windows, her hair and the pearls and her belly luminous. She still had that photo around somewhere; it was a favorite of hers. She took a photo of him naked, too. He was five feet ten, a very slim man with a raised appendectomy scar ("made by a butcher," he'd say) from when he was nine and a sharp, jutting elbow where he'd broken his arm and it had been set badly when he was ten. She thought he'd become a surgeon in order not to repeat with others the botched jobs done on him. David had curly black hair that he kept very bushy because she liked it that way—an Isro, they'd called it in those days. Afterwards, when he saw the photo of himself naked, he was delighted with how well hung he looked. They had made love slowly, gently, she on her side, her back to him because of her belly, still wearing her pearls, which they took off and hung from his erection for a moment, and she remembered feeling, in that city of churches, Jew that she was, beatified.

She occasionally recognized that she had an eternally summery image of her marriage to David. À la Fragonard, if that wasn't too fancy. It was not so much that the dead sprouted wings, as some said, for she genuinely believed David had been a good man—as was Stu. In fact, she was a fortunate woman. It had something to do, she'd had the thought very recently—why only very recently?—with glorifying the inaccessible, while denigrating what was available to her. She recognized in some inchoate way that doing this darkened her life, and the lives of others.

Afterwards, in that Toledo hotel room, she had asked him if he wanted to have anal intercourse, and he said if she wanted. Neither of them had ever done it before. She lay on her side and they lubricated him to the hilt and he came into her slowly, carefully, and it felt strange, like she had to go to the toilet. Throughout, she worried she'd crap all over the place. And she got angry at him later. And he said, rightly, "It was your idea!" And they both spent a long time in the shower.

Sometimes he would come almost as soon as he entered her. They would have screaming fights about it—why had she screamed at him? She had impoverished their love life—even though he'd get a second erection and could last so long she'd limp afterwards.

In a box from the basement she saw her shrink bills that he'd paid. She'd gone to Dr. Levinson with the complaint that she was in the wrong profession and that she'd married the wrong man. She'd had it with social work—sitting on the phone at the hospital trying to find dispositions for chronic psychiatric patients, getting them out of the hospital and into group homes, or into the homes of relatives. It often took days if the patient was poor. Finally, when she found a place, the patient would stay there at most a few months—after which he would stop taking his meds and end up hallucinating on the streets again. And then, back to the hospital. She wanted to do something less Sisyphean.

David made enough money so that she could afford to quit. She'd gone to film school at NYU, which she really enjoyed. But she wanted to be a star, to excel at something, and she never really had. Except that she'd been loved immoderately. But that wasn't exactly *her* excelling.

She complained that her husband wasn't creative. She should be married to a filmmaker. Not someone who put in long hours at a hospital, although he managed to drive Billy to school several mornings a week, and he ran a boys' basketball league. He spoke at different medical schools and hospitals, and not only about that procedure he had invented but about different materials he was experimenting with for pinning bones. She went to hear him a few times and was vaguely proud of him, but found the talks stupefying.

There was a receipt from a hotel in Lucca, in Tuscany. It had been pouring so hard that dark night that he had to pull the car to a stop on a cobblestone street before they could get near the hotel. Billy was asleep, seat-belted in, in the back of the rented car. She and David somehow got into a discussion of money. He was very proud of being a good breadwinner. She was maintaining that money didn't matter. Art mattered. She yelled at him, "All you think about is money."

"I'm what keeps this family afloat," he said. The rain beat

against the windshield and the top of the car. "It's because of me you can do whatever you damn please."

"Don't throw that up to me."

"I'm not. I was happy to pay for school for you."

"You don't respect me. I mean, as an artist."

"For God's sake, where do you get that claptrap from? Talk about *respect*! If I had to depend on you for my self-esteem, my head would be in the toilet."

She was in the bookstore with her son. Billy was his present age, thirty-seven, but with his formerly curly blond hair (a putto, they'd called him, until he was school age), indeed a big bush of curly blond hair, although his hair had never been bushy. Certainly he didn't have his current bright-brown wavy hair, graying a little, thinning out and receding at the temples. Instead of being distraught, he was happy. Happy to see her. In fact, he shone. He was well muscled, in a black T-shirt and red shorts. He showed her first editions of books she had read to him in childhood (he handled them with pleasure now, but also carefully): *Charlotte's Web*, *The Trumpet of the Swan*, *Norman the Doorman*. She remembered he would lie under the covers and she would lie above the covers beside him and read to him. They would look at the pictures. They would fall asleep together.

One night Billy, age four, had said to her, "Marry me."

"What about Dad?" She smiled.

"He can sew."

Now Billy took her by the hand and led her to his book-lined office. There was no photo of Lyria here, not even one with the glass cracked. And no computer. What there was,

was a riot of flowers, cream-colored roses on the desk, a tall black vase of burning orange gladioli standing in front of the fireplace, fat pink peonies and deep-red poppies in a bowl on a side table beside an easy chair. A soft light shone against the white walls. The mingled odors, the sweetness of the flowers and the woody acridness of the books, moved her. She and Billy slowly, languidly undressed, and he had a glistening erection. Her body was taut as a young girl's or as a pregnant abdomen. He entered into her and she came at once, explosively, yet gently, and they went on and on.

IN LOVE WITH MURRAY

In memory of Bernard Malamud

LEDA, A BUDDING artist, met Murray Blumgarten in the
late 1960s, when she was an undergraduate at NYU. It
was summer, she was working half-time as a salesperson at an
outré women's boutique, and in her free time, trying to paint
and attend as many art shows as she could. This afternoon
she was going to see what was happening at the Whitney
Annual. Tall, her pale blond hair piled high on her head against
the heat, she wore big carved wooden hoop earrings and
beads, and a (secondhand) orange miniskirt and matching
peasant blouse, without a bra. When she showed her art student
pass to the suddenly awake ticket taker, he waved her in and
nearly followed her into the elevator.

Somewhere around the middle of the show, which interested her mildly—there were the usual pieces, the usual styles:
op, pop, hard-edge, color field—she spotted a man she immediately recognized as Murray Blumgarten. He was standing
alone near one of his works, eavesdropping on visitors. It was
a huge, mysterious diptych of what looked like a sketchy,
ramshackle motel (was it the Lorraine?), a body on the balcony,
on the ground black men with agonized arms pointing in

different directions: a few pointed at a torn, blown-up black-
and-white-photo-like silkscreen of a dead white man on a
hotel kitchen floor, a Mexican busboy in white uniform and
chef's hat bent over him; others pointed at somber realistic
colored portrayals of police beating dying young men and
women and children outdoors at night. They were dying in
Central Park, for God's sake! Leda recognized the merry-go-
round—poles twisted, horses halved, quartered, shattered. Was
that Tavern on the Green, tables belly up, full of great shards
of glass? Blood was oozing, bombs were bursting off the edges
of his canvases onto the Whitney's walls. Leda hugged herself
in order not to be blown away.

"What do you think?" Blumgarten asked eagerly, seeing
that this lovely if overly-decked-out and under-corseted young
woman was stirred.

He looked just like his photo in *Art News*: middle-aged,
around her height—five feet nine—with light, ascetic bones,
his balding head covered by an old tan cap. His lips were
full, and he wore black-plastic-framed glasses, behind which
his fine brown eyes, his best feature, shone. His eyes caught
at you, felt you over, urged you out. They seemed now to
beckon the nineteen-year-old Leda.

"I hope you don't mind my impertinence," he said. "I ask as
one art lover to another, which I sense you are."

When she finally spoke, her voice quavered. "Yours are the
only works with a conscience in the show. And I love the different media—the oil, the charcoal, the collage, the metal . . .
The comment in *Art News* about your Jewish-merchant looks
was an anti-Semitic slur, don't you think? In my humble
opinion, and maybe I'm not being so humble, but you asked

for my opinion, you did—well, I think the only reason an artist of your caliber hasn't had a solo show at the Whitney is that you're not handsome enough to be photographed for *Harper's Bazaar.*" She couldn't believe she'd said so much. Had she made sense?

Murray grinned.

Was he flattered to be recognized? At least he didn't seem hurt at her flat-out statement that he wasn't handsome. He *wasn't* handsome, but his quality of attentiveness, so full-on, so direct, stood out like an erection.

So as not to seem a complete toady, she added, "But I do not find your paintings beautiful."

"No?"

She was surprised at his pained look.

"You don't see *any* beauty in them?"

In fact, his paintings were more than beautiful to her. She loved his sense of form, the way the tears in the silkscreen picked up the rips in the canvas, and the paint splatters continued over the edges of the canvas onto the museum wall.

At least no one else had heard her dumb-ass remark: the last visitor had left the room a few moments earlier. Oh, how could she ever make amends?

Seemingly recovering himself, he gestured good-humoredly at the walls. "Show me what you find beautiful. I'm interested to see."

On an inspiration, she lifted her blouse up over her face.

Sex with Murray: In the beginning she would lock herself into her bathroom and emerge wearing a hooded white terry cloth bathrobe, as if she were a prizefighter, her hair stuffed into the hood. She would take the robe off only under the covers.

"Is this my flasher from the Whitney? Is this my orange bird of paradise?"

"I am actually a very shy person." She held the bedclothes tight around her, although she felt silly, as if she were a child.

Murray was sitting up in bed wearing his eyeglasses, indifferent to his own naked body, his chest a motley thinning jungle of black and gray and white, the muscles of his arms and legs stringy. "Are you putting your diaphragm in down there?"

"Don't worry," she called up through the yellow-checked cover, her voice muffled.

"I'm not worried. I just thought maybe you wanted some help. I'm a dexterous type."

She shook her head. "I can handle it."

"I'd *like* to handle it." When she didn't answer, he said, "At least let me watch you handle it."

"The light's no good down here."

"Why don't you take the pill?" he asked, amused at her fidgeting.

"It's too new. I don't like messing with my body."

"Good for you!" He thrust his skinny arms forward in two triumphant fists.

Later he told her that he'd wondered if, beneath the covers, she was trying to signal him to keep his middle-aged haunches under wraps. But in her bathrobe, she would often undress him, teasing him by throwing his clothes to the not-so-far corners of her studio apartment. It was a slovenly place, art posters torn and taped askew on the walls, here and there dirty dishes and half-empty glasses with cigarette butts floating in them. Murray had an impulse to hold his nose. But the apartment had good light, and on the desk and hanging in the bathroom there were a few original paintings that showed talent—by her? She wouldn't tell him.

After two weeks, when she still had not shown herself, he roared, "Why do you deny a man who lives by his eyes?"

Arms and legs wrapped tight around him, she held him prisoner with her under the dark bedclothes. Tears tumbled out of her, and she dried them with the sheets. "I've only slept with boys . . . mostly in the backs of cars . . . I'm sure you've had models and mistresses . . ." She was wailing. "Mature women . . ."

"Oh my dear, my dear," he said in that old-fashioned, stilted way he had when he was moved. "I am less experienced than you think. Anyway, you are altogether lovely in my eyes. You need fear comparison with no one—"

"Not with the *Maja*? Not with the *Primavera*?" She couldn't stop wailing.

"But those are works of the imagination! Flesh made luminous by inspiration!"

"What about your daughters?" He had two grown daughters and a son. "What about your wife?" Finally, hot and sweaty but holding him fast, she belted out between sobs, "Your wife when she was young?!"

"Why bring my family into bed with us? Why torture us both?" He tried to lick away her tears, but she pulled her head back. "Who's been worrying you?" He wanted urgently to know.

"*Art News*. They said your nudes 'dizzied' the viewer,

'blinded' him, that they were 'salvos, starbursts'! I'll bet it was your wife when you first knew her." Leda groaned. "I've got fat pads over my thighs!"

"You exaggerate! You have what you're supposed to have. Your thighs are womanly."

"You haven't seen them!"

"I've felt them!" He grabbed the outsides of her thighs, kneaded them, pinched them affectionately. "Those—and these"—he gave her full breasts two smackeroos of kisses—"are the gracious cushions for my bony self!"

Even when the air conditioner gave out toward the end of that first summer, she would do it only under the covers.

"I'll cover you with my body," he told her.

But she clung to him and shook her head.

"My God! Who would have thought!" he exclaimed, when he realized she was still deeply uneasy not only about her shapely body, but about her whole young self. "I'll imagine you. I have a good imagination." He winked, then kissed her forehead and her eyelids, and said seriously, "And I'm patient."

Under the hot covers she was daring, licking him in places only his mother had touched before.

He wanted to reciprocate but was unpracticed, had come of age, he told her, in a sexually unadventurous time. "Is this your clitoris? Is this? Give me a flashlight, for Christ's sake. Why do you keep me in this dark shroud?"

As the cool weather came in, he got the lay of the land and, for no reason she could think of, she shed her bathrobe aboveground. He wept at her "gift" to him. Afterwards they sat back in the disheveled bed (Murray wanted to smooth and tighten the sheets but she waved him off), she smoking a cigarette and he drinking from a pitcher of ice water she had taken to keeping for him on the night table. He fucked himself dry with her, he told her happily, and, like a sea animal left out in the sun, had to reimmerse himself quickly. He had a golden cock, he announced with delight. He loved her.

Despite the twenty-eight-year difference in their ages, she turned out to have had more sexual partners. He had married early and had had children early and had made love with only five women in his life, and only one at a time, and he was curious and impassioned and grateful to her in his shyly arrogant way, claiming that in his late forties, she'd restored his youth to him. He'd spent his early years painting, always painting, and working to earn money—a necessary waste. "I deserve you," he said.

Murray was odd for an artist, an orderly, tense person who dressed conventionally if without concern for style, a man who rose at six every morning and did exercises out of a Marine Corps pamphlet. "That's as close as I'll ever get to the military, if I can help it." After exercising, he shaved and showered and rode his bicycle on a fixed route from the Upper West Side neighborhood where he and his wife had an apartment to his East Twelfth Street studio. On the way he bought the *New York Times* and read it over breakfast (a daily grapefruit and dry toast—once a week he permitted himself scrambled eggs) at the Olympia Coffee Shop on East Fourteenth Street. He folded his bicycle and carried it up to his third floor studio, where he unplugged the phone and taped his Do Not Disturb sign beside the doorbell, then worked for the next five hours wearing a large canvas apron over his shorts and undershirt and ever-present tan cap. He lunched out of a paper bag, drank from a small thermos of tea, and relieved himself into a Portosan he had had installed, there being no bathroom on the premises. When he was finished painting for the day, he would leave his studio like a patient emerging from a coma— lost, stumbling, eyes hardly open—and walk around the block, occasionally stopping to lean against one of the street's under- nourished trees. Afterwards Murray went back upstairs and napped and dressed in fresh baggy clothes, then set out to meet his wife at a museum or gallery—and, nowadays, to meet Leda, whom he presented to his wife as a promising student, a new friend.

Murray had a coterie of friends and he expanded in their company after the isolation of his day. There were several other artists in the group, as well as dealers and gallery owners and collectors who came and went and came. One distin- guished regular was an art critic who had won a Pulitzer Prize for his book of vignettes on the American art scene.

Leda was elated to be included among these shining men and women, but for her, Murray wore the crown. If they were at a museum, she would sometimes leave his circle to dash into an adjacent room where she'd copy down what Murray had just said. If the group moved on later to his apartment for drinks or dinner, Leda would excuse herself to jot notes in his bathroom. (Once Murray shot her a worried look, as though he feared she might be ill, but she shook her head vigorously, healthily.) His wife, Sigrid, a Norwegian scholar who taught medieval history to graduate students at Columbia University, prepared and endured these impromptu parties several times a week, although she seemed content enough when their grown children came—which was often—and

brought friends. Murray presided with relish over these min-
glings, as if water and minerals were coursing up his roots.

Alone at her apartment afterwards, Leda would pore over
her notes. Much to her surprise, at their next tryst she'd
often argue with him: "Who cares if William Blake said, 'The
nakedness of woman is the work of God'? Why not the
nakedness of man?" In bed she poked at his tendinous thighs.

"Leave my puny person out of this." Murray laughed at his
pale body. "The male physique has always been the glory of
artists—all that marvelous Greek statuary, Michelangelo's
slaves, his *David*. Do you have a book of Renaissance sculpture?" He craned his neck, but she shook her head no. "I can
see in my mind's eye Donatello's fetching *David*, slender boy
with a jaunty wreathed helmet. God, I'd like to take you to
Florence!" He looked suddenly, deeply sad. "You should really
be backpacking in Florence with someone your own age.
He should take you to the Uffizi, the Bargello. What are you
doing lying in bed with an old married man?"

"Middle-aged," she corrected him. "And I'll worry about
that, if you don't mind. You just keep on talking."

"If I give no thought to your situation, what am I worth?"

"Don't patronize me. Don't start in with the moral shtick."

He seemed to think about that, as if she might have a
point.

"I'm getting plenty out of this relationship," she went on.
"And you'll be the first to know when I'm not. Now tell me
about Blake."

He looked uneasy, but after a moment kissed her nipple.
"Anyway, I just think women were more Blake's type. Mine,
too."

She pulled her breast back. "And where did you come up with the idea that Picasso painted the families of clowns and circus folks because he wanted to 'ennoble the forgotten, accompany the lonely'? Maybe he just wanted to sleep with the clowns' wives."

"You really pay attention to me!" Murray grinned, settling himself against the headboard, an arm around her shoulder.

Leda shrugged. "You admire Van Gogh for not shooting himself sooner, you admire Monet for painting his water lilies even when he was nearly blind . . ."

He stuck his nose into her cleavage and breathed in deep, pressing her breasts against his nostrils. "I smell his water lilies everywhere."

"Would you know if something stank?"

He turned her over on her belly and ran his nose down her backbone toward her ass.

She giggled, and talked into the mattress. "No, seriously, you have a hearts-and-flowers view of the world."

Yet he was the first to admit they lived in a stinking century. One day he took her into the big downtown Barnes and Noble and bought her (besides many art books, one of them on Renaissance sculpture) Primo Levi's *If This Is a Man*, James Baldwin's *The Fire Next Time*, Simone de Beauvoir's *The Second Sex* . . . They lugged two heavy bags to her apartment, where Murray, all the while talking enthusiastically, placed each book in alphabetical order by author in her cinderblock bookcase. As they undressed, he was saying that the civil rights movement and the women's rights movement were the brightest glories of their black times.

"You're really into educating me, aren't you?" She was standing naked beside the bed.

"Do you mind?"

She kissed him with feeling. "I appreciate it."

He stepped away to look at her. "How I appreciate *you*!" He closed his eyes. "Your whole lovely self."

She knew she got ornery with him, practically kicked him in the shins. Kicking, arguing, she kept herself from feeling scared. Her longing for him scared her, as well as her gratitude for that longing. It scared her that she kept buying him presents— she who'd never bought a gift for a man in her young life. Men gave *her* presents. She bought him a brush now and again, a print by an unknown artist, and once a pair of gold cuff links, although he could never take her to openings, the only dressy affairs he attended. Murray begged her to stop spending her nothing earnings on him. (Although the print was good, the girl had an eye. And the cuff links, he didn't go in for jewelry, but these cuff links were wafer-thin, elegantly shaped, like a musical instrument, a piano, maybe, or a harpsichord, or some piano-harpsichord that had never existed before.)

His biking around the city scared her—in one dream a yellow cab hit him, in another a subway car, or maybe it was a cattle car—and she begged him to cut it out. (He wouldn't.) It scared her that the bony sight of him thrilled her, him just shambling down the street wearing that battered cap of his. Listening to Murray art-talk, she regularly creamed her underpants; in a taxi he'd felt her wet crotch once and couldn't believe the "generosity" of her body. Then she started worrying he'd kill himself fucking her—he was getting so little sleep—and even suggested, as a lifesaving measure, that they cut back. But he laughed in her face, which calmed her: making love she was (almost) sure that he loved her.

Two summers after the year Leda got her degree, the NYU art department was planning to show the work of recent graduates, and she wanted very much to participate. In the belief that his concentration and focus would focus her, Leda asked Murray to let her share his studio. She knew she had a tendency to get sidetracked easily—a friend needed a model for the morning and Leda would oblige, or someone asked her to help hang a show. Even buying a dress or finding a book might consume several hours of priceless daylight.

"No," Murray said.

"Why not?"

"It's my privacy, my solitude. My domain." He felt uneasy, knew he sounded pretentious.

Leda could not keep her eyes from filling up.

On the Friday of a week during which she'd showed up only once—Murray had acceded to a two-month trial—Leda arrived at the studio at twelve thirty in the afternoon. Letting herself in quietly with her key, she waved once guiltily at his busy back (they made it a rule not to speak if either was working), and then several times defiantly, as though she would break his concentration by perturbing the air. He did not turn around, and, almost relieved—she had nothing in particular to say to him—she changed into the dungarees and smock she kept on the chair in the corner curtained off for models.

Leda began squeezing paint out of tubes. With a palette knife she mixed several colors together, then tried out the new combinations on an old canvas with some ratty brushes. Pouring fresh turpentine into little pots to clean the brushes, she thought, what the hell, she might as well re-clean and soften up *all* her brushes—they had maybe stiffened some during their hard lonely week. Her hands reddened with her ablutions and seemed even to grow a bit puffy, but she kept on. From the neat pile Murray had stacked beneath the sink, Leda took clean folded rags and wiped the brushes down. She tried not to think of the good hour she had spent at these preliminaries.

At last she took the cloth cover off her canvas and stepped back. She shaded her eyes with her hand, then looked out through her spread fingers. She felt the canvas with her palms and fingertips. She went into the Portosan and sat down on the toilet.

At three o'clock Murray, deep in concentration and needing to pee, opened the door of the Portosan and found Leda sitting on the can with a flashlight reading.

She jumped up, although Murray had instantly slammed the dark door.

"I'm so sorry." He was truly flustered. "I didn't realize . . ."

He had certainly seen her pee before, so it had to be her reading that had agitated him. Watching her kill painting time was like seeing her shoot up.

"Not to worry." She tried to sound chipper as she pulled up her dungarees. "Coming right out." She emerged, the book behind her back.

She listened to his long urination.

Afterwards, while washing his hands briefly from habit

(they of course remained covered with paint), he looked at her questioningly.

She poked at the little piles of paint on her palette with the tips of her brush handles. "Why are you watching me?" she said.

Out of concern, with love, he wanted to say. But out of concern, with love, he said nothing, as though he were dealing with a sensitive adolescent from whom he must keep a respectful distance.

"Don't you have anything better to do?" she asked.

He resisted saying, I was going to ask *you* that, and simply nodded.

"Well, fuck off," she said.

His face darkened.

She blushed, but could not bring herself to apologize. As though it were a gun, she aimed her index finger at him.

Murray had an impulse to slap her, but he stood still, then lifted both hands in a mock gesture of surrender and, although it took him a while to regain his concentration, went back to work.

At four, after he finished for the day and cleaned his paint-flecked eyeglasses with turpentine and washed his sweaty armpits and chest with laundry soap, he asked her if she wanted to talk.

She was standing motionless in front of her easel.

"Maybe you want to walk? Hey, that rhymes." He smiled foolishly. "Look, I know you're not seeking advice, but the thing about painting is, you have to create a rhythm for it. It's rough if you work and quit, work and quit. You have to stay with it almost every day, if only for a little while. The quitting seems to check the flow, and then you have to break through into the rhythm all over again. Having a bad time at the beginning is almost necessary. It's a struggle and a struggle and a struggle, but if you keep at it right, the struggle can become a dance."

She burst into tears.

He held her by her shaking shoulders, swayed a little with her.

"I'm not your child," she said sullenly. They stood eye to eye. "I can't let myself depend on you as if I were your child."

"We all depend upon each other," he said quietly. "Let me see what you have there. I'm sure it's better than you imagine."

She shook her head no, but he had already turned the easel toward him. On the smeared canvas were dark wet stains— residue of turpentine—and occasional flecks of dull, dirty paint. And nothing else. She had erased a month's worth of fits and starts.

He stood beside her dumbly, almost as bereft as she.

During the next few weeks she refused to see him, rarely even picking up the phone, so that he was reduced to leaving notes with her doorman: "You can do it, dear. I have faith in you. Believe in your wonderful self."

And: "It's hard to believe in yourself in the beginning. At least believe in my belief."

He meant what he wrote, but the repetition made him sound evangelical (rabbinical, he supposed), hence suspect. In reaction, he sent her a silent bouquet of blue flowers, and then a drawing of a bouquet of blue flowers. He intended it as an unspoken promise that though she was blue now, she would flower—although he feared he'd gone from too obvious to too subtle.

He wondered did he sound selfless, as if he cared more about her art than about losing her. But he feared that he'd lose her forever if he didn't get her back to work.

"Look, maybe I've ceased being an inspiration to you," he wrote her. (Was the doorman delivering his fucking notes?) "What about the Art Students League? You need to be with people your own age."

She mailed him back a two-liner: "The Art Students League is loaded with old codgers. Maybe *you're* the one getting sick of dealing with me."

He thought she might have two points. He stayed away. Made love to his wife, which he did every so often anyway. She was not unwilling; neither was she enthusiastic. They were friends, there hadn't been passion between them for a long while, not for several years before he'd met Leda. Was Sigrid—dark haired, blue eyed, still a good-looking woman—having an affair? *Halevai.* It should only be. For a while before they'd met, she'd been with a woman; he'd once timorously suggested a threesome, but she refused. He hoped at least she wasn't having an affair with a student—that could be dicey, might blow her career wide open.

And her career was flourishing: she was writing her fifth book, she had been interviewed twice on PBS, there was talk of giving her a named chair at Columbia. He loved her enough to be curious about her, but didn't want to intrude, didn't want to stir things up. It was selfish of him, he knew: at all costs, he must not jeopardize his work. Which was going well.

But he couldn't get Leda out of his head. Was it only lust?

Well, there was that aplenty. But there was also a tenderness he felt toward her, he liked watching her bite into the brave new world, sour as it sometimes seemed to him. Was she his third daughter? But his daughters, dear as they were, were not artistic types. His world did not excite them. He frankly did not fully understand it, but he ached for Leda in a way that both pained him and made him feel alive. Was he old King David in love with Bathsheba? At least he hadn't had to murder anyone to get to Leda. At least not yet. He worked, wondered, and waited.

It was two months before she phoned, telling him to ring her doorbell, and then they fell on each other. He tried to hold himself back despite his urgency. She was silent and tense, and downed two glasses of white wine. When she finally came, she wept. "God, I'm a crybaby." He had an impulse, which he resisted, to cry with her. They napped deeply in each other's arms. Afterwards she brought out stale whole-wheat crackers and a lopsided chunk of cheddar cheese, the edges of which had hardened. At the thought of the feasts his wife served up, she was downcast. "I haven't gone shopping much. It's been a bad time." She paused. "I've been thinking hard about the trouble I have disciplining myself."

He tried to keep his eyes off her lovely breasts. The sight of the stiff pink nipples started his tongue gliding over his teeth, and—he was delighted to note, although his timing wasn't good—his cock rising yet again. She was an antidote to middle age.

"I don't want to sound like I'm on one of those daytime television talk shows," she was saying, "the ones where the contestants babble on about their troubles—you know, pop-psych shit. But I'm miserable when I'm not painting. Yet at the same time I have this impish feeling, this sort of glee. I don't know how to explain it, but it's as if I'm pulling the wool over somebody's eyes."

My eyes, Murray wanted to cry out. But he wasn't going to call attention to himself and his erection.

Lately he had had the frantic feeling she had made him into her jailer. Leave me out of it, he longed to tell her. But he kept silent, the blanket and his hands over his nether parts.

"Even my grade school teachers told me ad nauseam, 'Why don't you apply yourself?' As if I were paint." She laughed at her own meager witticism. "Look, I think I'm carrying on some kind of lifetime fight with my bossy mother."

Murray'd met the mother at graduation, a home ec teacher maybe five years older than he. Wearing small gold-stud earrings and a sleeveless black dress, she shook hands forthrightly— she had shapely arms—and thanked him when Leda introduced him as her professor. He felt uneasy about the deception, knew he would not like a fifty-year-old married man *shtupping* one of his daughters. Later he saw her mother lean over and whisper something, to which Leda responded with a vehement—in fact, an indecorously loud—"Will you let me alone, for God's sake?" The next day Leda told him that her mother had suggested she use the bathroom before the ceremony.

"You're probably thinking my mother's not so bad"—was the girl clairvoyant? what else was she aware of?—"and that I am one sick cookie and should maybe see a therapist." Leda held out her bitten nails and cuticles.

"I wasn't thinking anything. Of course, if you think therapy would help—"

"No money," Leda said.

"I could contribute."

"Ah, so you *do* think I need it." She wagged a finger.

He shrugged his exasperated shoulders. "I'm no expert. I know about paint."

"Anyway, I'm not from the talkers. I'll lick this. You'll see."

She did finish three good paintings that year, a reasonable if not exuberant number, and got two of them into the NYU show. Then, hoping that a new medium might make her pour forth, she turned to collage, and crafted out slowly and painstakingly four pieces (but only four) that were later hung in a gallery in Provincetown, "in the provinces," as she put it. Murray said she had reason to be proud: she was very young, and someone bought two of the collages, and she was mentioned a few times, favorably, in local reviews. Not everybody . . .

His career had meanwhile skyrocketed—he'd gotten his solo show at the Whitney, and several of his works had been bought by MoMA. Murray's fecundity was extraordinary for a careful man. He went so far as to quote *Lear*, "Ripeness is all," to show her there was nothing wrong with artists talking a little now and then, and also to assure her that her time would come. She had only to keep working.

Was she jealous?

Yes.

On an unseasonably hot day in May, Murray was driving Leda around the Hamptons in his wife's brown Volvo (Sigrid was doing research in more temperate Norway—alone?), the two of them looking for a bungalow to rent for a couple of weeks and drinking red sangria out of a gallon thermos— Murray abstemiously, Leda with her usual abandon—and fanning themselves with museum catalogues. On the back lawn of a large estate were bushes, twenty or thirty of them, bursting with lilacs. Nobody seemed to be around, and Murray cut a few sprays of lilacs for a still life. One white bush was stunning, the size of a young tree, but massive, and heavy with sweet, dense clusters of tiny white blossoms, and it had a pure radiance to it, a kind of shimmering white almost halluci- natory brilliance in the hot afternoon. They took a branch or two from several other bushes as well, their flowers exquisitely gradated hues of purple from palest blue to almost black, and just as Leda was about to get into the car—Murray was already in the driver's seat—she went back across that long long lawn in the heat to the white lilac bush and began cutting off more and more flowers, and then she started stripping the tiny blos- soms and shaking the branches with such force that the blossoms came apart and the huge bush seemed to be snowing itself and she tried to cut some more but she was so drunk by then and hot she could hardly handle the clippers, and she began ripping off leaves and branches with her hands.

Murray had to pull her away from the denuded, crippled bush. He hustled her into the car, fished some stained purple ice out of the sangria thermos for her cut fingers. "What's the matter with you? What is it?"

She felt anxious and frightened and heat dazed and watched him hurriedly cover the back seat and floor of the car with newspapers, then pile in the cut branches and flowers, and gun the car the hell out of there.

"What got into you? We could have been picked up for vandals—which we are." And he said something about a man his age carrying on with a child, he ought to have his balls examined.

It was getting toward late afternoon and he had her throw the rest of the ice from the thermos onto the lilacs. He bought more ice on the way home—"Are you trying to cool my brains?" she asked him—and she held some chips to her smarting fingers and some on her face and her eyelids and in her hair. But she was never able to tell him why she'd carried on, because she didn't know; and she laughed uneasily and they drove and after a while she fell asleep.

She awakened as he got her out of the car, walked her to her place, her throat dry, gut uneasy. He stood over her at the kitchen sink, insisting that she drink glass after glass of cold water to avoid a hangover—"Can't you learn to limit yourself?" And she drank shamefacedly, silently annoyed: You a puritan? A preacher?

That night she twisted the stems and leaves and flowers together and twined them through with clear picture wire and twisted it all around herself down her arms and legs and into a kind of gown or sheath and she looked in the mirror and began to feel better. And that was what she would wear with Murray to a big party that night in the Village—a pale-white silk slip, and then lilacs, mostly white, and nothing else. In the taxi on the way there he fretted aloud about having permitted her to leave the house looking like that—it was mad to go about half naked, even to a gathering of painters and poets.

"*Permit* me!" she shouted. "Who are you to *permit* me?!"

She was right, of course, and also he found her beauty so moving merged with all those flowers—and the white strappy slip was something like a (flimsy) dress, after all—that he was incapable, had she permitted him, of standing in her way. Unsubtle as her outfit was, God Himself was not very subtle— look at the Grand Canyon, he told himself, or even the leaves that blazed up every fall in New England.

For a while Leda went to work on her body. She gained ten pounds, she lost fifteen. Every few months she changed her hair color and plucked her eyebrows now this way, now that. He didn't understand why she was dissatisfied with her natural beauty, but he loved her, cymbals or cello. She modeled for him in all her manifestations and tried to let herself bask in the radiance of his attention. "Your soul glows in you," he told her once, and for weeks afterwards whenever she felt gloomy, she reminded herself of her lit-up soul.

How a man who never changed a stroke of his painting to please anyone managed to live a double life she didn't know. He seldom spoke about his wife—to protect her? Which *her*? She believed he rarely slept with Sigrid (once he let slip that she complained about his bad breath—Leda sniffed prodigiously, but detected nothing) although Leda imagined Sigrid accepted him dutifully when he (dutifully?) offered himself. Unasked, Murray told Leda twice that he would never leave his wife—her mother had died when she was four, and Murray did not think she could survive another abandonment. Hey, my father died when I was twelve, she thought to say, but didn't, she wasn't sure why. He also told her that in the

twenty-eight years since he'd met Sigrid, he'd nev\
anyone as much as he loved Leda. What Murray did \
Leda, although she had half intuited it, was that he was\
of her, of her dissatisfactions with herself, of her inabili\
organize herself, commit herself to her work in a thorough-
going way. He feared that he might somehow be undone if he
married her, his ability to concentrate destroyed.

She was hurt that he didn't ask her, although she half
believed she had never really thought about marrying
him herself—he was fifty-one now, and had liver spots on
his hands, and was growing ever more orderly. Was she a
star fucker? Yes. Yet she'd soothed him through a few bad
reviews—it amazed her that he was still so vulnerable to
them. Who were the reviewers anyway? Nobodies, she told
him, compared to him. Besides running errands and making
occasional mediocre meals, she had provided (and received
in full measure) steady honest admiration. Truth was, he was
the best company she'd ever known; going to a gallery with
him was like seeing with five eyes, her two and his three. He
was the background music of her life, and the foreground
music, although she knew she should be her own foreground
music.

Despite the tensions she carried within herself, and the tension that mounted now and again between them, there was often
a rush of days when they worked comfortably together in silence
and went their separate ways to meet later, a couple vaguely
undercover from the world and from each other, for a late supper
at some modest-or-worse Mexican or Chinese place his wife
would never frequent. And maybe he'd discuss a Topic with
Leda, say, the Jewish attitude to the painted image (although his

"raising her consciousness" had begun to grate on her) or they related (carefully) what they'd seen of each other's work that day and she'd be touched anew by how respectfully he listened to her criticism, as if she might also teach him a thing or two, which she might. Or they would go to the theater if he could get away in time, or to a concert—he loved music. And he felt bad he couldn't take her out in public more—his photo was regularly snapped nowadays—give her more . . . At least he would get her to a late-night movie, sometimes two, and then they'd come "home" and make love until three in the morning. He still had considerable sexual stamina and seemed able to awake refreshed after half an hour's sleep and ride his bicycle home.

Her few remaining friends asked her, though she asked them not to, how about babies, and a man who'd be there at four in the morning to change a diaper? And didn't she feel guilty toward Murray's wife, who was old enough to be her mother? She did sometimes, but mostly she tried not to think about her. It made Leda feel like a shit. Well, he was the one who should feel like a shit, not Leda.

One day when Murray was in Paris with his wife for an opening, Leda met a medical student in the emergency room where she'd gone to get a splinter taken out of her foot. As he leaned over her, the smoothness of the skin of his hands and the tightness of the flesh of his chin and neck affected her powerfully. In bed his taut shapely rump delighted her, and she never once closed her eyes, came with them wide open, so she could keep seeing him. Although she refused to go out with him again, she dreamed several times of his well-muscled thighs and upper arms.

Six months later, when Murray and Sigrid had gone to Barcelona for yet another opening—was he wearing the gold cuff links Leda'd given him? she didn't want to think about it—Leda picked up a young dentist in Washington Square Park. Well, he was technically a dentist, he explained to her, although not yet practicing—he was studying to be a periodontist. He wore shorts, and had swarthy, dark-haired legs and a lush summer wilderness of black hair that curled onto his shoulders. His name was Rafael, and Leda was sitting in bed kissing the forest on his head when the doorbell rang.

She was expecting no one.

Rafael suggested it might be a deliveryman who'd rung her bell by mistake.

She went naked to look through the peephole. It was Murray, and she felt panic, not only because here she was holed up with some hairy jackass of a dentist (not that she even knew if he was a jackass), but also because Murray was such a formal man, he would never appear at her doorstep without phoning. Some disaster must have occurred. Despite her berserk state and with one eye shut to see through the peephole, she examined his face as closely as she could.

But in his usual tan cap, he looked unusually, inexpressibly, happy.

After a while she realized that he was holding out in front of him a large gold-paper-wrapped package. Her impulse, even with Rafael in bed behind her, was to open the door and embrace him and tell him to come on in.

She mastered her impulse. Murray rang again. Had he heard her coming to the door? If not, he might simply go away and come back later. He knocked gently, and then forcefully. He owned a key to her place but had used it only once, when she'd gone home ill and slept through his anxious phone calls. If he did have the key with him, the door was on the chain lock, thank God. However, he would know she was in there, might even be able to see something through the open space, smell something . . .

What was that in his hands? It must have something to do with the look of rapture on his face.

He reached into his pants pocket and took out his keys. She stood immobilized, watching him.

The periodontist called from the bed, "Who is it? A deliveryman? Get rid of him."

She turned quickly toward him, a warning finger to her closed lips.

He added sotto voce, "On second thought, see if he's got anything to eat."

She tiptoed away from the door. "Get dressed," she whispered urgently. "You have to get out fast."

"What's going on? Who's at the door?" he whispered back.

At this point they both heard the key turn in the lock a couple of times, and then the door opened and Murray was calling through the spacious links of the chain lock, "Leda, honey, are you sleeping? Wake up, darling, wake up, sweetest. Have I got something to show you!"

To the young man in bed she whispered, inspired, "It's my father!"

Rafael, who was stepping into his jockey shorts, and pulling at the cloth to adjust his profusive self, whispered back, "Well, I hadn't imagined meeting the old man so soon, and under these circumstances, but I'm game." He hurried into his white athletic socks.

"Shhh. Don't make any noise. He's very jealous." She was about to add ominously, He has a real Oedipus complex, if you know what I mean. But she realized she had it reversed, and she feared she would soon start speaking total gibberish.

"Leda dearest, I have such a surprise for you!" Murray called from the doorway. He moved the door back and forth several times on the chain lock.

There was a fire escape out the back window and Leda pointed to it. Rafael, who went to the window, took one look down the seven flights and shook his head.

He stepped into his olive shorts and kelly-green body-builder T-shirt and stood, a tree, in the middle of her apartment holding his big sneakers. She thought of Murray on the other side of the door holding his big package. She feared her head would explode.

After a few minutes of pushing and pulling, Murray closed and locked the door—she looked through the peephole barely breathing—and pushed the elevator button. Rafael was tying his laces and as soon as she saw Murray disappear into the elevator, she grabbed her bathrobe and motioned Rafael out into the hall. She yanked open the door to the back stairwell.

"When will I see you again? I don't even know your last name." He was fumbling for his wallet. "Wait, I'll write my phone number on a dollar bill."

"Just tell me your phone number, my memory's excellent." She was pushing at his chest.

He was holding tight to the banister while reciting, slowly, the digits of his phone number. "Do you promise you'll call?"

"Yes, yes, yes . . ."

She had nearly closed the door when he yelled up from two flights down, "Do you remember my number?"

"I do! I do!" She repeated it rapidly, threw it digit by digit down the dark stairs.

"I'm Jewish," he yelled. "Tell your father I'm Jewish. Rosenberg's my last name. Rafael Rosenberg."

How did he know she was Jewish? The phone was ringing. She slammed the stairwell door shut, and ran back into her apartment and picked up the receiver.

"Did I wake you, Leda? Are you all right? The phone must have rung eight times. I'm sorry to disturb you, but wait until you see what I've got. May I come up? I'm right down here in the lobby. The doorman let me use his phone."

She tried to sound sleepy but she was breathless and she feared she might scream. "Just give me a few minutes, love." (She censored, Welcome home.) "I was napping. I was up late working."

"I'm glad you're working," he said. "I'll wait. I'll just stand right here beside the doorman and wait."

"Why don't you walk around the block?" she said. "It's such a nice day. I need a moment to clean up." She had actually grown a bit more orderly under his influence.

"I don't care how messy the place looks. I'm not a real estate agent."

"Walk around the block," she nearly shrieked.

She had the bed made, had gotten herself into her jeans and mussed blouse, put two barrettes in her hair, thrown the wine bottle in the garbage, and was hastily washing the wineglasses when he rang the doorbell. She looked quickly around, and seeing nothing more than usual amiss, opened the door.

Without saying hello, he handed her the package, his eyes full of tears.

She had a sudden fear he was crying because he had seen the young man leave. But how could Murray know where Rafael Rosenberg (was that really his name?) had come from—the building had twelve floors, several apartments to a floor.

Murray was pointing at the package.

She took it to the couch and they sat down together. After waiting a moment for her heartbeat to slow, she unwrapped the paper carefully. It was a thick coffee-table book, and there on the cover was a photo of a painting Murray'd done of Leda, Leda with ruby-red hair and a gilt halo and ruby-red bush, Leda as a stylized sacrilegious Madonna. Across the cover were the words of the title: MURRAY BLUMGARTEN: PAINTINGS DRAWINGS SKETCHES. Her own eyes teared up. After a moment she opened the book reverentially and saw that he had written in ink on the flyleaf *Leda Leda Leda*. And nothing else. She threw her guilty arms, still warm from Rafael, around him. Murray and Leda held on to each other.

Slowly, feeling hushed, she began turning the pages. On the first was a printed dedication, "For Sigrid, my wife, with love," and Leda thought that hardly compared with *Leda Leda Leda*, not for passion, but of course the dedication to his wife was printed and appeared on every copy. It was a declaration to the world. She felt suddenly a spurt of anger at Murray, but then she looked at the slack skin of his hands, their prominent veins, and she thought if she married Murray, she would be taking him to doctors soon (maybe to that medical student from the emergency room), having his blood pressure checked, and cooking special diets for him. Oh, that was ridiculous, Murray was quite vigorous, exceptionally so, for his age. For any age.

But was she ready to settle down at all, with anyone? There were men out there all over the summer streets—she looked out the front window and saw the acacia trees with their yellow feathery blooms in Washington Square Park—saw the young couples walking arm-in-arm, pushing strollers, saw dogs barking. Did she want to have a child with a man who could soon be a grandfather (one of his daughters had recently married), if she could pry him away, which was questionable, from his Sigrid, his wife, with love, with printed love? Leda continued turning pages, tears coursing down her cheeks, because she was young and not pregnant (not that she had ever really thought of becoming pregnant, only maybe when she saw paintings of the Madonna, although she had had a few scares which had fortunately—unfortunately?—come to nothing); weeping because the pages were paintings of her, not by her, and because she was sitting here with this man whom she adored, who was as much as, no, more a part of her than her dear inept father—she had lied only a little when she told whatever-his-name-was Rosenberg that Murray was her father. She cried for her young, stagnating life.

And of course at that moment the doorbell rang, and she opened it crying lavishly, and that ridiculously bushy-haired young man was there. "I'm sorry. I forgot my briefcase." He seemed to be speaking past her into the room, perhaps at Murray, who was sitting on the couch. "And it has all my perio notes in it, and I have an exam in the morning—" Suddenly he looked sharply at Leda. "You're crying—" He put his hand out, as if to touch her face. "What is it? What's happened?"

"Nothing." She tried to shut the door.

He got his shoulder up against it. "I need my notes, I'll be just a minute." He pushed past her to go down on his knees beside the bed. He reached under it and felt around—"I'm sure it's here"—and after a moment swept out his briefcase with obvious relief and stood up cradling it, along with a small dust ball, in his arms. "I'm leaving right now." He looked deferentially at Murray. "Sir, you have one sensational daughter there, you are indeed a lucky man." He held out a hand toward Murray, but Leda began pummeling the briefcase that Rafael Rosenberg held against his chest, propelled him backwards a step or two toward the door. "I hope to be meeting you again, sir, soon, under the right circumstances." He whispered to Leda from the doorway, "Are you sure you're all right? Call me." She got the door closed, but not before he blew a kiss into the air.

Leda stood rigid. Murray sat on the couch, his open book a boulder in his lap. His face was gray, and for a moment she feared for her life.

"Who are you?" He had to repeat himself because she couldn't hear him.

She mewled, "It's me, Leda," as if he really didn't know. She felt like a small child. She repeated her name. Then she said, "I'm whoever you want. Only don't leave me."

"Whoever I want, and whoever *he* wants, whoever he is. Does he matter to you? At least tell me he matters to you." Behind his glasses, his brown eyes were red.

She feared something had burst in him.

"No," she said. "I don't know if he matters to me. I just met him today. Yes, he matters to me, if you want him to."

"Are there others?" He was feeling around the couch as if he were a blind man feeling for suitors.

"No," she said. "Yes." She swallowed hard. "One. A year ago. Nobody matters but you." She clutched at his shirt.

Finally his hand came upon his cap, which seemed to be what he was looking for. Gripping it with his fingers, he groaned and stood up.

"Don't go," she begged. "Don't leave me."

He looked dazed, standing beside the couch. When he finally began to speak, he spoke very slowly, as though he were himself trying to understand what he was saying. "He's a young man. Of course. Your own age. Is he married? He's not married. Tell me he's not married."

She shook her head. "I don't think so. I don't know. What's that got to do with anything?"

He stood with a fist clenched to his heart. She feared he would smite his chest.

"Sit down," she said. "Stay here."

"I've driven you to—to—" He knew what he was saying was true, and suddenly he wondered why he was being so dramatic. "But why shouldn't you? I've told you, again and again, though evidently not often enough. There's my wife, my children . . . I should have expected . . . I *did* expect . . ." And then he cried out, "But I can't stand it!" And with what strength he had left, he lifted his book off the coffee table and hurled it out the open front window.

Neither of them moved for a moment. Then Leda got up to see if he'd killed anyone. Looking down, she saw a hole in the front first-level awning. But no one was lying on the side-walk, traffic was not at a standstill, the chess players were still playing in the park.

She moved away from the window and mastered the impulse to go down in the elevator and rescue her book. "No, no," she said, as much to herself as to him. "You've driven me to nothing. I've loved you of my own volition. I've never loved anyone but you. I never *will* love anyone but you." And she burst into tears, because she feared she was telling the truth.

"Shhh," he said. "I'm a selfish old man. Kept you locked up. Made you sneak around, when of course you have every right."

He was shuffling around the apartment, looking at what he knew by heart—his drawings of her naked on the walls, two collages of hers, on the table a blue faience hippopot-amus she'd bought at the Metropolitan Museum, the peach-striped bedspread they'd purchased together—as though he'd never seen them before and would never see them again.

He walked out the door, one hand tracing the doorknob. "I've wasted your time, your precious time."

"No, no," she cried in the hallway. "You've made my time precious, made my life precious," she yelled at the closing elevator doors. Although the elevator was descending, and had now reached the fifth floor, the fourth—she watched the numbers light up and then darken—she shouted, "I revere you!" Alone in the hall she leaned against the elevator and wept.

He called the next morning. "I ask your forgiveness for my histrionics, to say the least."

"Where are you? Come here, let me give you a cup of tea, a glass of water."

"I need to get hold of myself," he said.

"I'll be faithful. Please. No one else matters to me."

"You mustn't be faithful," he said. "I need you to be faithful. I've done you a grave injustice."

"I love you," she said.

"I love you, too," he groaned. "I thought I was enough for you. What an egotist I am! You deserve a husband, children, a life."

"Oh, don't be so conventional, I deserve *you*," she said. "Why can't we just go back to the way things were?"

"Impossible." After a long pause he said, "I'll be in touch, but not for a while."

She left a number of impassioned letters at his studio without getting any response, and one terse practical note: "I'm only twenty-three. I've got plenty of time for babies."

He mailed her a *New Yorker* cartoon of a scuba diver retreating from a beseeching mermaid at the bottom of the ocean. "Of course I love you," the caption read, "but I'm running out of air."

Two months later he sent a postcard from a show of his in Williamstown, Massachusetts. "My host here is a poet, sensitive gray eyes, an even-featured, gentle man. Really a lovely person. If he hadn't been married, I'd have brought him home for you."

She didn't believe him for a minute.

A month later he telephoned to discuss her future. Could he help her get into graduate school, not that she needed help. What were her plans? Was she short of money?

She thanked him, but she wasn't interested in graduate school. She wanted to see him. "Don't ease your guilt by offering me money. You're insanely jealous. I promise I won't do it again. Just come over here!"

Instead he sent her a book, note enclosed. "Read Chekhov's 'The Lady with the Pet Dog.' It's about what begins as a vacation dalliance between Gurov and Anna, unhappily married to others. It ends as a passion that dominates their lives. In the last pages Gurov realizes that love is a burden, almost a doom."

He sent her another note. "Give the book away. You are a young woman. You are not unhappily married. Go out. Have children. Thrive!"

She went out but did not, could not, fall in love. "There is only you," she wrote him, since he refused to see her, afraid of himself. She read about openings of new shows of his, and thought about attending, dressed all in black, and taking a knife to his canvasses. Once she saw him at MoMA with his retinue of followers. She couldn't hear what he was saying, but he was laughing and gesticulating. Leda slunk away.

She developed a strange depression: the world lost its color and texture and shape; people seemed about to evaporate; only noise remained, car horns, sirens, the blast before the building falls. She came down with sinusitis and then a low-grade intractable diarrhea, so that she was literally weeping out all her openings: she had turned into a husk, a pod, and wouldn't have minded blowing away.

And then in the end Murray accommodated her, freed her, she told herself, although she knew it was bullshit. His wife called Leda early one morning, before it was on television and

in all the papers. The previous night, at age fifty-three, at a
dinner party at his apartment, Murray stood up to toast a
Rothko painting in the living room and collapsed back into
his chair dead.

AT THE HAPPY ISLES

"PUSH ME," GUSSIE Fernmann Klein tells her daughter, Marilyn, who has been pushing her in her wheelchair from her second-floor apartment into the elevator and is now pushing her through the ground-floor lobby toward the dining room. It is noon, time for lunch. Some of Gussie's fellow residents at the assisted-living home are assembled in the lobby, where a gas fire burns in the fireplace. Marilyn assumes they eat second lunch at one thirty. The residents are mostly un-made-up and gray haired, although a couple of women have thin bright-dyed hair teased out into bouffant hairdos, through which you can see scalp. Gussie's hair is blond with gray roots, in curls that she tightens down every night with bobby pins. She wears green eye shadow and a gay red lipstick, some of which she has rubbed onto her cheeks. Around her neck is a shiny gold necklace, to set off her powder-blue polyester pantsuit. "Push me faster. Take me to the dining room."

Gussie, at ninety-nine, is one of the oldest residents at the northern New Jersey facility, although she tells no one her age, and she insists that Marilyn keep it secret as well. Gussie doesn't permit Marilyn to tell her *own* age, either, because people who know Marilyn's age may be able to figure out Gussie's.

Marilyn is sixty-eight. *Her* hair is dyed two tones—a double process, they call it at her expensive Manhattan hair salon: dark blonde, with light-blonde highlights. Otherwise, she doesn't take any special care of herself—sometimes she remembers to use moisturizer on her face. But she is a pleasant-looking woman, fair skinned with a straight nose and her mother's large hazel eyes. A little overweight, she tends to wear black often, including today, with the idea that black is slimming.

In the dining room Gussie points—"I want to sit *there*"— and Marilyn moves a chair away from a table for four and rolls Gussie into its place. There are perhaps fifteen other tables of various sizes. At the center of each table are purple anemones and pale-yellow Gerber daisies—fake flowers, but good fakes. Marilyn once had to feel the petals to make sure they weren't real; the flowers sit in clear vases, with fake water levels.

On this Saturday afternoon the house is moderately full; while some residents are out with family, others have visitors. Most of the diners are elderly women, but here and there a few men are sprinkled around like pepper on a salad. In their noses several people wear plastic tubing attached to gray metal oxygen tanks set up beside them.

"Hellooo," Gussie calls to a heavy black waitress who is taking orders at another table. (The residents are mostly white, the kitchen staff exclusively black.) "My daughter's here. She's come all the way from New York. She's a medical doctor. Bring us some menus."

Although Gussie has publicly announced her daughter's profession again and again during the years she has lived at the

Happy Isles, Marilyn still feels embarrassed. She rolls her eyes and shakes her head and aims her words at no one in particular: "Who cares if I'm a doctor!"

Gussie wears two hearing aids but does not seem to hear what her daughter is saying.

Eight years earlier, when she began having trouble carrying her groceries up the outdoor brick steps to her duplex apartment, Gussie insisted that her daughter help her move to the assisted-living home in West Orange, New Jersey, where Gussie had brought up her children and worked as a fifth-grade public school teacher and head of the glee club. She chose the Happy Isles because three former female colleagues lived there. In the beginning, Gussie kept her car and drove it over the familiar roads to buy stamps at the Main Street post office, shop for small items at the Essex Green mall, or take "the girls" to faux-rustic Pal's Cabin for a hamburger and an ice cream sundae on a summer evening. Sometimes at one of these destinations, a former student, often with children or grandchildren in tow, would recognize Gussie—"Aren't you Mrs. Fernmann?" or "Aren't you Mrs. Klein?"—and make a fuss over her, which Gussie would relate to Marilyn with delight. But as her vision and hearing began to fail, she had to give up the car. Two of her teacher friends died, and the third moved to Florida. Now Gussie keeps to herself and seems to know the name of only one other resident, Betty Berle, whose son is an orthopedic surgeon. (Gussie needs a hip replacement, but at her age major surgery is not an option.) Occasionally Gussie will say, "See that woman over there? She's a Christian lady." Or "See that woman walking by? She's cuckoo." Gussie circles one finger in the air beside her ear.

"What have you been doing lately?" Gussie now asks Marilyn, who reaches over and takes her mother's gnarled hand. Gussie's fingernails are silver polished, but some of the silver has worn off. She wears a wide gold wedding ring with tiny, multicolored stones.

"Well, I've seen a few good movies."

"Big deal. Hellooo!" Gussie calls again at the waitress, who is still taking orders at the other table. There are eight people sitting there, several of whom have had strokes and cannot speak clearly. "Wait on us, miss," Gussie yells. Her voice starts to crack as if she will cry. "Give us a couple of menus. For God's sake, help us out!"

Several residents turn to see who is making the commotion. Marilyn takes her hand away from her mother's. The waitress hurriedly brings over two menus, and Marilyn thanks her. "Mom," Marilyn says. "What about *puh-lease*! And *thank you*?!" But the waitress has already returned to the other table.

"Order whatever you want," Gussie tells her daughter. "It costs me the same if you order one dish or five dishes. Take the soup or juice to start. Which are you having? Get the soup. People rave about the soup."

The manager stops by to ask if he can place another resident at the table. For this particular meal, the resident has no one to sit with, he explains; two of her friends are in the hospital, another is at a granddaughter's wedding.

"No way!" Gussie says, grimacing and turning her head side to side vigorously. "No how! I'm with my daughter who drove here an hour from New York City. She's a medical doctor."

Marilyn winces but remains silent.

The waitress shambles over in the director's wake. Marilyn orders decaf coffee and a cheese omelet. Gussie says to the waitress, "Bring us two vegetable soups."

"I don't want soup."

"You'll see it, you'll want it."

"I'll blind myself." Marilyn smiles.

When the soup arrives—the waitress brings two—Gussie says, "Look at all the vegetables in it."

Marilyn keeps her hands in her lap and looks determinedly away.

Gussie blows on a spoonful of soup. In bringing the spoonful to her mouth (Marilyn worries for a moment that Gussie will bring the spoon to Marilyn's mouth), Gussie loses her grip and the hot soup ends up in her lap. "Damn it to hell!" Gussie yells out. "You bumped the table!"

"Shhh, Mom. I didn't do anything."

"You most certainly did."

"No, I didn't."

"Yes, you did."

Marilyn leans over and cleans the soup off her mother's pants with a napkin. For a moment, she imagines she detects some unpleasant smell, some foul odor drifting near her mother. Has the woman farted? Perhaps it is only the odor of her hair permanent. Marilyn sniffs discreetly near her mother's hair—nothing—then tries to put whatever it is out of mind as she dips her mother's napkin into her glass of water and rubs at the stain that is left. Marilyn wonders if she *did* bump the table.

Suddenly three emergency medical technicians, two young men and a woman, enter and stride to the far end of the

dining room where a man sits limply in his chair. Their youth
and quick gait make them particularly smart among the faded
flowers of the residence. Marilyn would like to go over to see
if she can help. It would make her feel more like herself—she
heads an emergency room at a large Bronx hospital. But she is
not at her hospital and she doesn't want to interfere with their
work. Also, her mother might resent her getting up and going
to the rescue, so to speak—would she look on it as an abandonment? Or would Gussie be proud of her? She still cares
what her mother thinks, Marilyn notes ruefully. She continues
eating her omelet as the medics take the resident out on a
stretcher.

Her mother says, "They come for that old coot every week.
He's wheezing or gasping—always something with his breathing. Calls attention to himself, if you ask me. How're your eggs?"

By saying they are good, Marilyn feels she is making some
admission or doing some obeisance, but they are good and she
says so.

At this point, Marilyn takes out a little "airplane bottle" of
wine from her pocketbook. (Two days earlier she was flown to
Atlanta to give grand rounds on the initial management of
head trauma in the emergency room. She couldn't resist pock-
eting the wine, a business-class freebie.) Marilyn unscrews the
cap, pours herself a little and tastes it. Potable.

"What are you doing? Is that *wine* you're drinking?"

Marilyn considers claiming it is grape juice, but telling a lie
seems cowardly. "Yes, Mother, would you like some? I'll split
it with you."

Her mother waves her hand in a dismissive gesture. "You
need that? You need to drink in the middle of the day?"

"Mom, it's a single glass of wine. And I'm happy to give you half of it."

"And you a doctor! You should know better! What kind of example are you setting?"

"Mom, it's red wine. The latest medical opinion is that red wine is good for you."

"I watch TV. You need to drink a thousand bottles of red wine for it to be good for you."

Her mother is right. Marilyn sips a little more. "Look, Mom, we discussed this already. Remember the fight we had last Christmas? I had one glass of wine! You said you wouldn't make a stink about it ever again." Marilyn, who drinks maybe a glass of wine a week, is beginning to feel like an alcoholic.

"I don't remember anything about Christmas. It's a goyish holiday."

"Mom! We've been celebrating Christmas every year since I was born!"

"Well, it's enough already! Are you ashamed of Hanukah? And why do you have to drink with *me*? When you know it annoys me!"

An occasional drink with her mother might make their meals more festive, Marilyn had thought—the food here is generally not flavorful—but perhaps the drink also serves to calm her down. Should Marilyn really need calming down after so many years? And if she *does* still need it, why not just take a tranquilizer? She is sure she has some old ones in her apartment. Or she can get a colleague to write her a prescription.

Suddenly it occurs to Marilyn that, more than the need to soothe herself, the glass of wine smacks of defiance! After all, what has she had, three glasses of wine with her mother in the past year? And a fight over every one. But isn't it unworthy of Marilyn to drink merely to show her mother that she, Marilyn, can do what she damn pleases, despite her mother's disapproval? At age sixty-eight, shouldn't she already know she can do what she damn pleases? Marilyn hears herself say, "All right, Mother, since it bothers you so much, I'll drink only half a glass."

"Why drink any, why drink even half a glass since it bothers me so much?"

It is a point. Hardly magnanimous, but a point. Marilyn looks longingly at the wine. Then she asks herself, what is she doing carrying on a battle with a ninety-nine-year-old woman? "Mom," she says. "I'm here to visit you. I'll do whatever makes you comfortable."

Her mother gets a glint in her eye as she shifts her focus to Marilyn's omelet. "They say eggs aren't so good for you either, but what the hell. Do you know one of my husbands used to serve me breakfast in bed, often an omelet? I forget which husband. I had three wonderful husbands. I only tell people here about two." Gussie lowers her voice. "If they knew I had three, they'd be mad with jealousy. No one had better husbands. Even their mothers all loved me."

Marilyn has heard many times about her mother's three husbands—the second was Marilyn's father, a good-hearted, boyish traveling salesman who used to sell men's ties for a company called Beau Brummel. The third, her stepfather, was a quiet, self-effacing owner of a small business that made automobile seat covers; although Marilyn never warmed up to him, he paid for her college and medical school without a murmur.

Gussie rarely discusses her first husband, whom she'd known since grade school, an accountant who died of cancer at the age of twenty-five. Marilyn has never asked her mother how she felt about his death. In those days you didn't question your mother, or you didn't question *that* mother. Gussie had been a no-nonsense, sure-of-herself person. As a little girl, Marilyn had thought that she couldn't die if her mother was in the room. Marilyn had also believed that her mother would never die—and it was turning out to be the case.

With her crooked fingers, Gussie picks the white meat out of her sweet-and-sour chicken. "Did I ever tell you how after my first husband died, his mother got sick and she would only let *me* give her her medicine? She felt everyone else was trying to poison her." Gussie smiles.

"Yes, Mom, you've told me that many times." Then Marilyn adds, "But I don't mind hearing it again."

"What? What did you say?"

"It's lovely his mother loved you so much."

"My grandmother lived with us when I was growing up. Did you know that?"

"Yes, Mama."

"And she didn't let me go to kindergarten. She wanted me with her. So I missed kindergarten. Did you ever hear of anything like that?"

"She certainly loved you, too."

"Yoo-hoo," Gussie calls to the waitress. Gussie makes a large arm gesture beckoning her over. "Order the ice cream," she tells her daughter. "They have terrific peach ice cream."

"It's fattening, Mom. I shouldn't have it."

"You *could* stand to lose some weight. You have a fat *tuchus*.

Do you use any wrinkle cream on your face at night? You have more wrinkles than I do."

Marilyn smiles sadly.

"Well, get the sugarless ice cream. It's also very good."

"It's still fattening."

"Start a diet tomorrow. Why are you always on a diet? You never lose any weight. Do you have apple pie?" Gussie asks the waitress. "I'll have apple pie with some peach ice cream on top. What'll you have, Marilyn?"

"I'll have decaf coffee."

"That's all? Bring her some sugarless ice cream. Bring her chocolate."

"Mom, chocolate makes my face break out. You know that."

"Still? At your age, your face still breaks out?"

After lunch, Marilyn pushes her mother to the elevator. Marilyn's arms and back ache, and her neck is sore.

"Hit two," her mother says in the elevator. "Come on, goddamn it, I'm on two!"

Marilyn is suddenly, unexpectedly, screaming. "You've been on two for eight years! And I pushed the button before you opened your mouth!" Marilyn closes her eyes for a moment, upset with herself. In the ER she will yell at a nurse or doctor who endangers a patient, and she is not above yelling at an adult friend who gets on her wrong side, but she tries never, anywhere, to yell at children or at the aged. Oddly, she seems to have trouble regarding her mother as aged.

"It's good when you talk loud. I can really hear you," Gussie says.

In the apartment Marilyn gently helps her mother out of

the wheelchair to sit on the couch. She has a small two-room apartment with good light, but the overstuffed, heavy wooden furniture her mother bought for the Victorian house Marilyn grew up in is out of place here. Even back then, Marilyn felt overwhelmed by the furniture, dreamed once as a child that she lived in a dark forest inhabited by a witch. Her father, whom she'd adored but considers lightweight in retrospect, had sometimes teased her mother by carrying a flashlight around the house; yet he let her choose everything, including the color of Marilyn's room—dark green, which she hated. Gussie directed him all the time, even when he drove to his own mother's house. Often he'd quipped, "I want to go *my* way, the *wrong* way," and he occasionally called her "sergeant" or "captain." But Marilyn cannot remember her father ever making a real ruckus about Gussie's domineering ways. Maybe he socked it to her in private? (Marilyn hopes.) As for the furniture, she has offered to buy her mother a new, more diminutive couch and chairs, but her mother thinks it would be a waste of money.

In the living room there are a few photos of Gussie as a young woman, with dark, dramatic hair and glowing eyes. There are also photos of Marilyn's father—she still finds him handsome, with his fair skin and blue eyes—and a few of Gussie's last husband, Jack Klein. From Jack, Marilyn has a twelve-years-younger half brother, an obstetrician, who is married with three grown children. That whole side of the family lives near Chicago.

So the care of Gussie falls on Marilyn, Marilyn who never married. For ten years, she had loved Huang deeply, a tall, handsome Chinese American neurologist who had been a teacher of hers. His wife, from a village on the Yangtze River, had a terrible case of multiple sclerosis; and Marilyn and Huang, who was patient and highly ethical, planned to marry as soon as the wife died. But she stayed alive—she was alive still, institutionalized—and he died after an auto accident. Marilyn was at his bedside. He died apologizing to her.

If she'd only had the nerve to become pregnant by him! Years later, she adopted—a Chinese infant who is now twenty, a student at UC Berkeley. Mi-yay studies Chinese and has spent the last two summers in Xian with her birth mother. Marilyn believes this is a good thing, but she also feels abandoned and jealous, although she disapproves of these emotions.

"Did I ever tell you how your stepfather asked me to marry him?"

"Yes, Mom, you have."

Gussie leans across the couch toward Marilyn in a confidential way. "Well, Jack and I were in the kitchen drinking coffee and he says, 'Gussie, I want to have sex with you.'"

Gussie's hearing aid begins to whine. The sound is high pitched, grows louder. Scowling, her mother turns and twists the device a few times in her ear.

Marilyn, pleased to have the story interrupted—perhaps Gussie will forget about it altogether—says, "Let me take a look at that, Mom." Her fingers itch to do something, even if it is only to get her thumbnail under the latch that opens the plastic door so she can check the battery.

Her mother takes the hearing aid out of her ear and, holding it in one hand, slaps at it with the other.

"Mom!"

"You keep out of it!"

After a few more slaps, the pink fetal thing stops squealing. Gussie puts it back in her ear and smiles. Marilyn is astonished.

"So like I said, Jack and I were cozying up to each other in the living room, on this very couch"—she touches the velvet material, which is midnight blue; Marilyn has at least managed to get the worn slipcovers replaced—"and he says to me, 'Gussie, I have to have sex with you.' And I say straight-out, 'Sorry, I only have sex with men I'm married to.'

"'All right, Gussie,' he says. 'Then we're getting married—right away.' And we did—the next day."

How much of this story is fabricated? As an eleven-year-old, Marilyn had fought back tears at the wedding—her father had been dead less than a year. It was held at a synagogue, and her mother had her hair done up with reddish streaks and wore a fancy wine-colored dress with décolletage. There was a crowd and a big white cake, which said CONGRATULATIONS GUSSIE AND JACK! How could it all have been put together in twenty-four hours? And had her mother really never slept with Jack before? Marilyn had come home a couple of evenings from Girl Scout meetings and found the front door chain locked; she'd waited quite a while in the cold for her mother to open it.

Does Gussie talk about her three husbands incessantly because Marilyn has never had any? And the story of refusing to have sex before marriage, is that cooked up because she suspects Marilyn of having affairs, which Gussie disapproves of?

Marilyn *has* had a few affairs, one before Huang, several after, although not immediately after; she even had a brief fling with a woman, an inhalation therapist working at a nearby hospital. But Marilyn is discreet around her daughter, perhaps too discreet. Lately Mi-yay has taken to saying, "Mama, go out! Stop clinging to that one dead Chinese dude! I don't want to bear all the responsibility for you!" (Marilyn wonders, a little bitterly, what responsibility the girl thinks she is bearing out in Berkeley and Xian. Although Mi-yay is entitled to her own life.) But Marilyn has never again experienced the passion she felt for that one dead Chinese dude.

In some ways, it has been a lonely life. Her work keeps her blood flowing—she has no intention of ever retiring—and her daughter has given her joy. Gives her joy.

Then she thinks her mother, of course, must be lonely, too. Perhaps it is paranoid to imagine there is some competitive motive behind her mother's stories; perhaps her mother is only recounting past glories, even confabulated past glories.

"Let's play gin," Gussie says, and Marilyn gets up right away to take the cards out of the desk. They often play during Marilyn's visits. Her mother is still sharp at cards, so usually it is a real game. They both enjoy it. Lately, her mother has unwittingly taken to tilting her cards and Marilyn can see them if she doesn't dutifully avert her gaze. Today Marilyn feels she has to win, and if it takes looking at her mother's cards, so be it. During her mother's tilt, Marilyn sees that her mother has two kings; Marilyn sequesters her lone king, which she would have discarded had she not seen her mother's hand. The knock is ten or under. After a few picks from the deck, her mother discards one king. Marilyn does not know whether she should pick up this king, counting on her mother to discard the third one so Marilyn will have a set. Her mother always throws out high cards, understandably, when the knock is high. So Marilyn picks up the king. Her mother then takes a card from the deck and knocks, using the third king as her knocking card. Marilyn is stuck with, among other cards, the two kings, which are worth ten points each. Her mother wins by forty-one points, a sizable victory. Gussie grins widely, exposing two stubs of teeth in the dead center of her lower jaw and a few empty spaces on the sides where molars used to be. Marilyn, angry at herself for losing so roundly and even after cheating (serves her right!), wonders when was the last time she took her mother to have her teeth cleaned.

Looking at that jack-o-lantern jaw, Marilyn has to remind herself that as a child she thought her mother very beautiful. When Gussie was out of the house, Marilyn would often sneak into her mother's bedroom (she never thought of it as her parents' bedroom, although, of course, it was) to try on a see-through nightgown or a pair of high-heeled strapless shoes. (Marilyn does not want to look down now at her mother's wide black orthopedic shoes.) And she remembers Gussie, whom she'd disdained as a teenager for having "no intellectual interests"—which was not inaccurate—once explaining "The Love Song of J. Alfred Prufrock" to her when she was home on college break and having trouble writing a paper on modernist poetry. Impressed and momentarily humbled, she'd asked her mother, "How did you understand that?"

"Oh, it's just from living and loving—you'll catch on as you get older."

Now Marilyn collects the rotten cards and shuffles them.

Gussie continues looking very, very proud. "You may be a fancy schmancy doctor, but I'm still a better cardplayer!"

"Well, we're not finished yet," Marilyn responds. She is surprised at how churlish she sounds.

"So what's new with my granddaughter, Mi-yoo, Mi-yay? Why didn't you name her Miriam or even Mary?" Gussie is still beaming. "How is she? Way out there. Any chance she'll become a doctor?" From the lamp table she picks up a pearl-framed photograph of Mi-yay, one of her in high school, ice-skating in a lemon-colored short tulle skirt and long-sleeved silk top. She is trim. Her black hair is pulled back in a tight bun and she has a concentrated, happy look on her face.

Marilyn tries to sound nonchalant, although she is still irritated. "Oh, Mi-yay's fine, Mom. I don't think she wants to be a doctor. She's considering majoring in Chinese literature. Maybe she'll become a doctor of Chinese literature."

Gussie waves dismissively, her gold ring glinting. "What can you do with Chinese literature? You can't make any money off of Chinese literature."

Marilyn is dealing the cards. She counts and recounts them to be sure she hasn't given her mother an extra card. Then she remembers she *has* to give her mother an extra card. Marilyn lost the last hand, so her mother gets to discard. "Maybe Mi-yay will become a professor. A professor of Chinese literature."

Gussie is positively gleeful. "A professor at Harvard!" Neither Marilyn nor her brother got into Harvard undergraduate or Harvard medical school, to Gussie's chagrin.

Marilyn waits for her mother to pick up her cards and arrange them and discard. This takes Gussie a considerable while these days. Marilyn herself doesn't have two cards that match. She is disgusted. She gets up and turns on a lamp beside her mother so Gussie will see better.

Years ago, when Marilyn wanted to adopt, Gussie was adamantly against it. "No one will marry you. Who wants a forty-eight-year-old woman with an infant? With a Chinese infant!" It was then that her mother told her something she'd never revealed before. While Gussie's first husband lay dying of cancer, Gussie was pregnant. She found a "doctor" in Newark, and there, for three hundred dollars (she'd bargained him down from five hundred), in a dark back room, on newspapers, she'd had an abortion. Marilyn has wondered over the years, should she have thrown her arms around her mother? But Gussie had not looked sad. She seemed to be presenting her action as practical, indeed exemplary behavior. *Marilyn* had certainly felt sad, but she had also felt angry and manipulated, blindsided.

Gussie never gave her approval for the adoption, but she bought the layette and paid for a year's worth of Pampers when Marilyn returned from China with Mi-yay. And had Macy's deliver baby intercoms for every room in Marilyn's apartment. Later, Gussie went to ice-skating meets, insisted the girl be bat mitzvahed (Marilyn left it up to her daughter, who declined), and, in her wheelchair, attended Mi-yay's high school graduation.

"I have to go to the bathroom," Gussie suddenly yells, dropping her cards.

Marilyn quickly helps her mother move from the couch to the wheelchair.

"Come with me!" her mother cries out.

"Why?"

"I need you to pull down my pants!" There is anxiety, almost panic, in her mother's voice.

"Mom, since when do you need help with your pants?"

"Hurry up! Push me!"

"I'm pushing you!"

In the small bathroom Marilyn puts the brakes on the wheelchair so her mother can lean against it to stand up. Then Marilyn shimmies down her mother's slacks and yanks down her underpants, but she is not quite fast enough. Some loose beige-colored stool splats out onto her mother's buttocks and the back of a thigh before her mother turns and manages to land on the toilet seat. Gussie's face contorts and whitens around her lipsticked cheeks. A volley of explosive sounds emanates from her. The bathroom is instantly malodorous. Gussie leans over and grabs her loose belly.

"Are you all right, Mom? Are you all right?"

Gussie is grunting, lost in concentration. Or is it pain?

Can Marilyn leave the bathroom? Wouldn't it be kind to give her mother some privacy?

But her mother may need her.

After a few minutes Gussie straightens up. She pees voluminously. Marilyn is trying to breathe shallowly. Although she is no stranger to blood and urine and feces, and she sees many people unclothed in the emergency room, almost none of whom are lovely, she does not want to see her mother's scrawny, veiny legs and nearly hairless pubic area.

What is wrong with her mother? But Marilyn knows that a little incontinence in someone her mother's age is not unusual.

As her mother wipes herself, she gets a yellow-brown streak on the right sleeve of her pale-blue pantsuit. "Damn!" Gussie says. Grabbing some more toilet paper, she tries to clean her sleeve with it, but she is awkward with her left hand and succeeds only in soiling her fingers.

"Hold on, Mom, wait!"

Gussie takes more paper to clean her fingers and ends up with both hands besmirched. "Get me out of here!" she yells, grabbing on to one of the armrests of the wheelchair. There is now a faint yellow-brown blush on the dark armrest.

"Don't move! Stay put, do you hear me?!" Marilyn's voice is higher than usual, almost as shrill as Gussie's. She wants to call for an orderly, or a nurse, but she is not at her hospital.

"Where are you going?" her mother cries out, nearly rising from the toilet.

"Down to the front desk!" Marilyn says in what she hopes is a commanding tone. "There must be someone who can give us a hand."

"No, no!" Gussie whispers. "Don't tell anyone, do you hear me?"

"Mom—"

"Don't leave me!" Gussie howls. She waves her arms in the air.

Afraid her mother will clutch her hair or pound a dirty fist against the wall, Marilyn moves away from the door and hurriedly returns to the stinking bathroom.

Gussie reaches for her daughter's hands.

Marilyn backs away in the small room.

"Shush!" Marilyn says, not meeting her mother's eyes. Confused and uneasy, Marilyn tries to turn the volume down. "Don't touch anything," she says—quietly, she hopes. In her mind she hears herself singing, "Everybody loves a baby, that's why I'm in love with you, shitty baby."

"What? What?" Gussie yells. She claps her hands twice, as if for a servant. "Just get my pants up. Get me out of here!"

The microscopic fecal cloud her mother must have created with each clap!

Marilyn explains, as from a very great distance—although she is only (still) two arms' lengths away, standing with her calves up against the cold bathtub—that she will have to clean Gussie, change her jacket, maybe her underpants.

"I'm not dirty!" Gussie cries out. "I'm your mother!"

"Look at your hands!"

But Gussie bucks up and down on the toilet seat, one hand on the wall, the other on the sink for leverage. "Get me out of here!"

If Marilyn has to wrestle with her, how will Marilyn clean her up? How clean herself up? Marilyn sees two naked women struggling in the mud.

"Where are you going?" Gussie whines.

From the kitchen Marilyn gets a pink plastic bowl and half fills it with warm soapy water.

"What are you doing with that?"

Marilyn explains slowly and, she hopes, patiently, as if she were talking to two-year-old Mi-yay—she is trying for an almost crooning tone—how they will both wash their hands for starters, just put everybody's hands, four hands, twenty fingers, in the soapy water. "Remember, Ma, how you taught me—after the toilet—wash-uh, wash-uh, wash-uh." Marilyn puts her own hands in first. How will she wash the woman without gloves? Ah, it is her mother!—and keeps singsonging to her. Gussie looks doubtful, but after a while allows her hands to be moved into the water. "Rub-a-dub-dub," Marilyn says. "You used to tell me that." Did her mother tell her that? Marilyn even manages to get her mother's nail brush off the sink counter and into the water.

"That's enough!" Gussie suddenly screams, and Marilyn realizes she is bruising her mother's thin skin with the brush and slowly, regretfully, throws it overboard. Rinses her mother's hands and pats them dry. Then she gets her mother's arms out of the jacket and drops it into the sink and turns on the hot water.

"You're ruining my suit!"

"Shh, shhh, little dear," and then, inspired, Marilyn sings, "Mama's gonna buy you a mockingbird. And if that mockingbird don't sing, Mama's gonna buy you a diamond ring."

"Who the hell are you talking to?" Gussie slaps a clean hand out at Marilyn but misses her face, barely grazes her shoulder. Gussie slaps out again, but Marilyn has quickly backed away. Her mother sits sputtering on the toilet in a blue sleeveless cotton shirt, the flesh of her upper arms dangling, a few wisps of gray hair hanging from her armpits.

Careful to keep out of striking distance, Marilyn washes the armrests of the wheelchair—Just whistle while you work, she thinks but doesn't sing, although she does give a little whistle. "Up now, Mother, come on, dear, stand up." As they both know, once Gussie is up, she will lose her balance if she lashes out. She stays seated. Marilyn stays standing behind the wheelchair. Finally, half clacking her tongue, half whimpering, Gussie slowly, jerkily, rises and leans against the armrests so Marilyn can wash her butt and thighs. Wipe her mother's asshole until the sponge comes away clean. "Clean as a whistle," Marilyn beams, showing the sponge to her mother.

Gussie goes silent.

Marilyn gets the slacks and underpants off over her ankles and shoes, leaving the underpants to soak in the sink, although it is possibly overkill—no, there is dried shit on the waistband; when did that get there?—helps her mother into clean underpants from the dresser. Marilyn's sure hands are unsteady. After inspecting the powder-blue slacks, she pulls them up over her mother's legs and gets the elastic waistband above her mother's belly.

Should she hire an attendant for her mother? But how can Marilyn afford that?

She lays a sweater over her mother's bare slumped shoulders, then helps her get back into the wheelchair and gives her a little push out of the bathroom.

Marilyn sprays the toilet seat with disinfectant, sprays the air in repeated vigorous lunges as if she is attacking mosquitoes. Then she washes her own hands, washes her arms up to the elbows nearly the full length of time that surgeons must, though she longs to run from the room. Then she rubs soap and water over the shoulder of her jersey where her mother slapped her, even though she is almost sure her mother's hand was clean. Any minute, she expects Gussie to yell from the living room, "What are you doing in there? Are you here to visit me or what?" But there is no word. Marilyn finds one yellowish fecal fingerprint on the wall and scrubs at it, cleans the sink, then washes her hands again briefly. At last she leaves the bathroom and closes the door tightly behind her.

Her fingertips are water wrinkled. Half-moons of sweat glisten on the underarms of her black jersey. She feels vaguely tremulous.

Some fancy schmancy doctor.

But she is not displeased with herself.

She sits down in a heavy armchair facing her mother. Gussie does not look at her. After a few minutes, Marilyn asks in what she hopes is a matter-of-fact tone, "How long has this been going on?"

No answer.

What is the right way to put it? "How long . . . that . . . you can't get your pants down . . . by yourself?"

Gussie keeps a fierce silence.

"Mom?"

In a sudden rush, Gussie cries out, "I can't walk. I can't hear. I can hardly—pull down my own pants!" A tear comes out of one eye. "And other people can dance."

Marilyn goes to her mother. She touches the tear on her mother's cheek. She squats down and kisses her mother's forehead lightly. Marilyn can still smell the odor from the bathroom and she feels suddenly like putting a cloth over her nose, as she has seen people do on the TV news when they are looking for dead relatives among a slew of bodies massacred days earlier.

Will her own daughter feel the same way one day? Will she ever have to clean her up, and in what humor will Mi-yay do this? Will she even be there to do it?

And Marilyn wonders for the first time, unbelievable that it is for the first time, how much longer will her mother live? For a moment she feels profound grief, and then she is aware of a wish to get it over with, to get Gussie into the ground.

Marilyn envisions reaching into her pocketbook for the Swiss Army knife she keeps there. And still bending over her

mother—perhaps it will look as if she is embracing her—
Marilyn might punch swiftly through her trachea, hack at
both carotids. Bright blood spurts wildly out of Gussie, who
gasps, gurgles, looks disbelievingly, malevolently, at Marilyn.

Marilyn moves the cards aside and helps her mother
flop onto the velvet couch. She hands her mother her cards.
Marilyn will discuss the attendant with her brother the obstetrician, who is wealthy but stingy. She will push him to split
the cost with her.

They play two more games of gin and Marilyn does not
cheat. Her mother wins one, Marilyn wins one.

DANCING

One

I AM SITTING in my first-period class, Calculus AB, which I signed up for because I'm lazy. The really genius kids, and there are a lot of them here, take Calc BC, which would have been a shitload of work. But maybe I should have done it because I am sitting in class feeling bored and trying not to look as if I'm staring at the really knockout breasts of Gina Pappadopolis (her face is lovely, too, but if you look at someone's face, they notice faster) or just plain dozing off. The teacher is making diagrams on the board and yada-yada-yadaing and even though I know it won't be great for getting into college if I don't ace this mother (which I should be able to do with my eyes shut), unfortunately, my eyes are shut. My mom is starting in on me about college these days. "You're a junior and this year counts and it would be masochistic of you . . ." She's a psychiatrist, my mom is, you could tell? And maybe she feels she has to keep nagging me so I don't think she's stopped being my mother and become my dad's full-time nurse, which is all right with me, her being his nurse, my father needs her.

As I said, I'm sitting in Calc AB supposedly trying to pay attention but I have this perverse feeling, what with my dad and all, I just don't give a fuck. It is a beautiful day, clear and warm, and I want to be outside—not looking out at downtown Manhattan or even across at Gina's boobiful boobs. (She's very smart, and popular, and aloof, at least she comes across to me that way. Also a kind person. At Stuy—Stuyvesant High School, this hot-shit public school in New York City that you have to take a test to get into but the hype is better than the school—Gina started the Big Sib program, seniors looking after freshmen.) Anyway, she is looking intently at the board and taking notes, while I have put my pencil down.

Suddenly everybody feels the building shake and the teacher looks at the students for a minute as if they did something and a couple of kids actually look at each other and roll their eyes like maybe they went a little too far this time and then the teacher shrugs his shoulders and tells everyone "Pay attention" and goes back to writing quadratic equations on the board. And everyone pays attention because everyone's mother is nagging them and most kids at Stuy don't need anyone nagging them.

I think I actually fall asleep for a few minutes because when I open my eyes and look out the window, I see something that I never saw before. There is an immense fireball two thirds of the way up the North Tower of the World Trade Center, red and orange flames bursting out of the building, out of some kind of huge living hole, and I think, what is this? I never saw a big fire up this close before! Just a few blocks away. It is startling and horrifying and beautiful, and I want to tell everyone in class to come over to the window and take a look, what could be going on? But I can't get myself to disrupt the class because I want so badly to disrupt the class. Still I can't stop looking at this humongous fire and then I hear sirens, which you hear a lot in the city, it's no big deal. But this is one fucking fire, and that building must be full of people, everybody at work, a lot of people are going to get hurt, this is not an art exhibit. Smoke starts across the bright blue sky. Kids are talking in the hall outside, which you don't hear much at Stuy, and now nobody is paying attention to the teacher at all because everyone is staring out the window. And then Mr. Lee, the teacher, this pretty unflappable Asian guy (well, Asian American), is staring out the window, too. "Good God!" he says. One lone man at the bottom of the big hole is waving a white handkerchief. I can't see his face but I know it's a man, that's how close we are. And I get this nauseated feeling because clearly people are trapped right in front of us and we can't do anything. The teacher yells, "Everyone stay put, I'm going to find out what's happening," and he leaves the room fast. Somebody thinks to turn on the TV and we all see the World Trade Center on fire on the TV and on fire out the window, and a newscaster says in an awestruck voice that a plane has hit the North Tower of the World Trade Center and then they show the plane hit the tower. I know it can't be an accident because I have been in the cockpit of a Cessna 172— my dad and I took some lessons when I was thirteen before he got sick, it was very cool—and so I know that you don't hit the World Trade Center on a clear day unless you intend to, and I feel frightened and enraged. Meantime, an assistant principal comes on over the loudspeaker and says in a wild voice that a plane has hit the tower, and to stay calm. Everyone should go to their next class. And the bell rings to change classes and nobody moves and then at the burning building the man waving the white handkerchief stops waving it. He climbs up across debris to the edge. And he jumps. A few people gasp. Somebody screams. Then there is silence in the room except for the TV. Nobody moves. Everybody is milling around outside in the hall, you can hear them, and one kid in class says, Did you see that, did you see that, and nobody else says anything. I am swallowing and swallowing. New kids start coming into the room, some of them joking and laughing, and one of them is saying, Can you imagine those sand niggers flying into the World Trade Center? And another says, We ought to nuke Mecca. But nobody in Calc AB says anything, and we all get out of the room fast and quiet as if we committed a crime.

In the hall I see Sam, a friend of mine, who is pushing the buttons on his cell phone, really banging them, and I remember Sam's father works in the World Trade Center and I think should I say something. What's to say? A girl I was in *Pippin* with last year, Elena, is crying with two other girls I know and we all hug for a minute and I say I saw this person jump out of the building and they say what, what and nobody can believe it. Nobody can believe anything. Mr. Lee is in the hall hurrying back to class, and he stops and puts out his hand and we shake hands very gravely and I want to tell him, I want to tell an adult about the guy who jumped but I can't say it again and I go down the hall and to my next class thinking I should have said something. Mr. Lee is a good guy and I am trying not to think how hot it must have been for that man to jump forty floors, fifty floors, a hundred floors, instead of waiting for the fire department. Not even my dad in the situation he's in would ever do a thing like that, or I don't think he would, though I wouldn't blame him.

My next class is AP Physics taught by a real jerk, Mr. Walsh, and he says something unbelievable about how if you use position vectors you can calculate the velocity or the route or something about how the plane hit the building and he starts pulling the shade down and says we're going to have a lesson. One of the seniors says you must be kidding and another turns the TV on and the teacher turns it off and another kid turns it back on and the teacher says he'll send him to the principal's office and while they're arguing we hear this rumble, which is not on the TV and the lights in the room dip and the TV goes staticky and two kids pull up the shade and in a second there's another fireball as big as the first one and this one is coming out of the South Tower and then we look back at the North Tower and now you can see more people at the windows of the North Tower. High up in the North Tower. Above the hole. Above the fire. On top of the building. That's probably where Windows on the World is, a fancy restaurant and nightclub where my parents go dancing every year for their anniversary. People are standing up there waving. Are they workers from Windows on the World? At this hour of the morning? It's almost as if they're waving at us. One fellow in the class starts waving back frantically. And then a woman jumps. And then a man. One kid opens up his arms, he holds his arms out, and then he puts them back down by his sides. Another man takes a woman's hand and they jump together. A girl starts to sob. Another man jumps. And another. Each time a person jumps, people in the classroom scream. And

Mr. Walsh closes the shade and he doesn't say anything. Two
kids rip the shade off the wall, which is an act of tremendous
violence, and those kids are going to get into the worst trouble,
and I try to concentrate on the trouble they'll get into as if
that is real and the people jumping are unreal and two girls
have their heads down on their desks. On the TV, the planes
are hitting the Twin Towers again and again and I wonder
what other buildings are hit, is all of New York on fire, is the
whole country on fire? But the TV is showing only the World
Trade Center buildings on fire. You can see it better right out
the window and you can't see the people jumping on the TV.
More and more people are watching TV and not looking out
the window. The announcer talks about terrorists and Arabs
and a few kids look at Khalil Rasheem, an olive-skinned,
large-brown-eyed kid who always acts dignified, and he holds
his head up very straight now too but he doesn't look at
anyone and he doesn't look out the window either or at the
TV and you can see his black hair is wet on his forehead. We
hear seven airplanes are on the loose, only four accounted for,
the Pentagon hit, and the White House is hit, and the announcer says who knows what will be hit next, the Empire
State Building, the George Washington Bridge. That's where
my father is, the hospital is maybe ten blocks from the George
Washington Bridge, and I know right away I have to get out
of here, my parents have enough to worry about without
worrying am I all right, I don't want my father to have a heart
attack. And I try to borrow a phone from the kid next to
me who is punching the buttons and I explain my dad's in the
hospital I just blurt it out, this thing I haven't told almost
anybody but now of course no one pays attention and after a

while the kid gives me the phone and I either get busy signals or no dial tone or anything. I run out of there down to the first floor where there are four pay phones but droves of kids are trying to get to them. I use another kid's cell phone—no luck—and then I make my way up the stairs toward the third-floor exit that leads you out through an overpass over the West Side Highway. I figure I better just leave and take the subway up to the hospital—are the subways still running—or else I better start walking. My mother's probably going there too if she's not there already but there are so many kids with the same idea and the guard won't let anyone out. You can see through the glass walls of the overpass the West Side Highway down below nearly empty, no traffic. There are always cars and trucks zooming up and down and now some ambulances and police cars are racing downtown, and nothing else. I figure I'll try a different exit. So I go back through the overpass into the building and downstairs two floors to the front door that faces south but a guard is there, too, the regular guard, George, a big black dude, he is blocking the doors with his body, and he looks pretty panicky himself. He knows me. I had told him a little about my dad because the guard's mother is sick, too, with diabetes, she had her leg amputated.

He won't budge.

Sorry, man, he says.

And over the loudspeaker another assistant principal is saying in a preternaturally calm voice to proceed to homeroom.

I go to homeroom. It's on the ground floor, and as soon as I get in the door, the first thing I do is look out the window. You can't see the towers from my homeroom, and I realize all at once this is fine with me—I don't want to be a journalist or anything—what you can see is this street going downtown. And just as I get to my desk there is a long fierce roar. Everybody looks at the TV and the tower is collapsing and out the window suddenly debris is coming down and the bottom of the South Tower must have collapsed down like a sand castle, all this crap flying around and everybody is suddenly backing away from the window and the visibility has gone to zero. All we can see is what's on TV, that South Tower coming down and down, the announcer saying hysterically the tower is collapsing, and this huge dirt cloud and the North Tower still standing with this awful fire in it. One tower. Like the world is out of balance. And then a lot of banging noises and I wonder are the windows popping out of the school? Or are those gunshots? And all the students move far away from the windows, they stand against the wall by the door. Maybe after five minutes we hear on the loudspeakers the principal telling everybody to proceed slowly to the north exit of the building, they are going to evacuate the building. We are not in any present danger, but everyone has to leave. It doesn't take a genius to know that we are in very present danger. Because if the North Tower goes down and it doesn't collapse straight down like the South Tower seems to have done, then who knows how it will fall, and if it falls uptown we are in plenty present danger and everybody just starts walking out of the room and down to the north exit. Hundreds of kids. And nobody runs. There are retarded kids and kids with cerebral palsy who are suddenly also down on the ground floor in their wheelchairs. (I vaguely remember there's a special ed class on the seventh floor. How did the teachers get them all down to

the ground floor? There are only four elevators.) Their teachers are trying to get them out in an orderly fashion and one of
those kids is flailing his arms around in his wheelchair like he
is a windmill and he is laughing and laughing. Another is
wailing and smacking himself on the ears.

The teachers keep telling the students to move slowly,
deliberately, and orderly and not to trample anyone but I don't
see anyone trampling anyone not even the retarded kids are
trampling anyone although later there are rumors that a few
teachers ran away and the principal ran away but I didn't see
anything like that.

Finally I get outside and I start up the paved pedestrian
walk by the Hudson River, hundreds of kids are walking pretty
fast up that walk north, and a few kids have cameras and are
taking pictures of their friends with the World Trade Center
burning behind them and this kid Jake I know from American
History asks me do I want a picture of myself and I say no. A
couple of people are listening to portable radios and telling
others what they're hearing. "No one can find the president,
or the vice president. They're in hiding." And somebody says
that asshole Bush, he should have been in hiding since the
Supreme Court stole the presidency for him. And a few people say "Right on!" But it dies down pretty fast. Then all at
once Gina Pappadopolis is standing next to me, she is walking
right next to me and I don't know how it happens but suddenly
we are holding hands very tight not looking at each other
but walking next to each other pretty fast north. And I almost
want to slow down thinking this girl is holding my hand
which she would never do if the world weren't ending, and
I want it to end as slowly as possible and I am worried is my

hand clammy. I can hardly believe anything. There are businessmen and women (anyway, people wearing suits) running,
really running, past us, all dusty and a few have their briefcases
with them, which is weird, and one guy has a bloody cheek.
Gina runs over to help the guy who is bleeding but he just
shakes his head and keeps running. And she comes back and
takes my hand again like it's normal (!) There are two firemen
with their black rubber coats full of chalk and one of them is
asking for water, his face is streaked black, and I give him my
water bottle without letting go of Gina's hand and somebody
asks what's happening and the fireman doesn't answer. I look
back and I see what's left of the World Trade Center white
crud coming out of the sky and litter and dust and dirt all over
everything and I think for those people down there it must be
like Pompeii when Vesuvius erupted. We start smelling smoke
or imagine we are smelling smoke and one of the guys with a
portable radio says we are not under attack a plane has gone
down in Virginia or Pennsylvania, the White House has *not*
been hit—one kid yells "Damn!"—and I just keep walking
fast uptown next to the river and there are helicopters overhead and two big guys from the football team are running
next to us and I nod at them and wonder do they know Gina
do they see her holding my hand but they are in much better
physical shape and they are moving really fast chatting with
each other like they are out on a run trying to get in even
better shape and they lose me and Gina one-two-three. Most
of us are happy because we are all together. I keep seeing kids
I know, and girls, especially from the plays I've been in, keep
coming over and hugging me but I don't let go of Gina's hand
and a few people are scared and we are all a little scared at the

same time that we're laughing and some kids keep looking downtown full of pity for those people. At Houston Street students start leaving in packs and Gina says she lives nearby do I want to come to her house and I try one more time to get my parents on the phone, Gina's phone, and I can't. But I can see the George Washington Bridge uptown. It looks all right but very far away and I know I have to get there.

So I tell her I hate to leave and will she be all right and can I take a rain check or a terrorist check or whatever kind of check there is in the world nowadays and she kisses me hard sort of half on the cheek and half on the lips and I kiss her back hard but we don't use our tongues and she darts away and I am alone or no one I know is around for a minute and I am in some kind of ecstasy at the same time as I can see smoke across the downtown sky.

I keep on thinking about Gina and the farther I get from downtown the quieter the streets are: people outside eating ice cream talking to each other and there is no traffic anyplace. It's like Venice where my parents took me when I was ten and I remember that you heard footfalls and human voices and water and not much else. And I keep on between the park and the Hudson River all the way uptown another three hours and I am thinking what would have happened at Gina's house if I'd gone there would her parents have been home does her dad sit in the house and write all day like my dad does? Like he used to.

I arrive at the hospital. There are many ambulances outside the Milstein Pavilion, and police, but I don't see injured people. The ambulances are empty with their motors running. I go up the elevator to the ninth floor where my dad is and it is very quiet on the floor no one bustling around, no nurses, no orderlies except you can hear all the TVs going so I knock on my dad's door and yell at the same time from outside that it's me and I'm fine and I open the door but I don't go in because I'm sweaty and dirty, and what with my father immunosuppressed. My mother runs out and we hug like mad even though since I've been thirteen I don't ordinarily like my mother to hug me it makes me edgy and my father comes to the door all hooked up pushing his IV pole with no hair and grinning. Then his eyes go wet. I know it's with pleasure at seeing me. But I feel if the whole world has changed, why hasn't my father changed, why does he still have these IVs in him and the pole and no hair and why are his eyes wet.

Two

In the middle of the night Matt sits in his hospital room, leaning his forehead against the window. He wishes the cool feel of the window against his skin were also clarifying, but it isn't. What is out there? Trying for a longer view, he slides his chair back—very, very quietly; his wife is asleep on a cot the nurses have kindly found for her.

Beside him, hanging from his IV pole, are two transparent pouches of liquid, one clear, the other faintly blue, both dripping slowly down into plastic tubes that insert into a catheter that has been implanted in his chest and threaded into his heart. The label on one pouch reads VINCRISTINE, the label on the other GANCICLOVIR. Both are marked POISON! over a diagram of a skull and bones. "Who does the PR for the hospital?" Matt quipped the first time the bags were attached to his pole. But he has been living with these and similar bags for five months now—CYTARABINE! CYTOXAN! VP-16!—and he doesn't pay them much mind.

What he is attending to so closely, what he is trying to get his best bead on through the window, is the George Washington Bridge. It has always been a source of comfort to him. Substantial, indeed massive, it is *there*, always there. When he wakes in the middle of the night and is unable to get back to sleep, it is brightly lit, and there is a kind of purity, even sanity, to its white lights, the pale-blue lights, a reliable healthiness, although that may be pushing it. Even in the middle of the night there is life on it, always somebody coming or going, so he tells himself why not one day him? He has always wanted to drive cross-country. And while he finds it hard to believe he will ever again have enough padding on his bottom to endure the jostling of a prolonged car ride, still he can picture pressing his foot down on the gas pedal, Ann sitting beside him, an atlas of the country in her hands, their son, Solly, in the backseat leaning forward to listen to rap on the radio, which will change to country and western and who knows what else as they move farther west. Yes, Matt can see himself driving across this bridge, sticking his head out the car window (after all, it is just another window) and looking down the Hudson River, down toward the Statue of Liberty. Or he'll wave an arm out the window, maybe both arms, what the hell, wave them at the world (Ann can steer), and yell at the top of his lungs "Yippee-ay-yay—yippee-ay-yay—yippie-ay-yay!"

He closes his eyes for a moment and when he opens them the bridge is gone and he gets a tight frigid sensation up the back of his neck. What is going on? If the bridge had been hit, he would have heard something. Still, he looks down at the river to see if the bridge has fallen in, if parts of it are jutting out of the dark water. After yesterday morning, anything can happen.

Slowly, his eyes accommodate, and he sighs with relief, for yes, despite its unwonted darkness and apparent desertedness (is that a single pair of headlights coming toward him, tiny, tiny, as if the two minuscule lights were suspended in black air?) and its muteness (well, it is always hard to hear the sounds of traffic through the thick unopenable hospital windows), yes, yes, the bridge is nevertheless *there*. Perhaps there is a problem with the electricity; much has been understandably chaotic today. Actually, now that he reflects upon it, might it be intentional that the bridge is dark? Didn't Londoners black out their whole city during the Blitz and didn't they survive? The police must be letting almost no one pass. Perhaps those tiny dim lights belong to an ambulance or a fire truck. The lights are moving very slowly, scarcely moving. Perhaps the vehicle is being stopped at various checkpoints. Has the National Guard been called out? He wishes that he were standing on the walkway watching what is going on.

Looking out the southern window—his hospital room is small but it is a corner room with a window on each outside wall—he sees much of the city stretched out before him. New York is white-lit but subdued, he doesn't see any Great White Way and he doesn't see the Empire State Building, which is usually lit up, often red, white, and blue. (The Empire State Building was not hit; no, he would have heard, he has been watching TV all day.) But the city is not dark on the whole.

What is missing, he realizes now, are the many, many white headlights of cars, bright goggle-fish eyes coming at him. There are a very few white lights, a few red taillights, perhaps an occasional car is allowed through on official business, or perhaps they are all ambulances. He suddenly realizes that there is no need for the authorities to black out the city, or to black out the bridge—the enemy has no airplanes (if we have just the one enemy), they can only hijack ours. And ours are no longer moving, the government has closed down the airports. So perhaps the darkness on the bridge is unintentional, not part of any plan. But if the Empire State Building is dark, and the bridge is dark, then maybe there is a plan. They are trying to protect us.

Squinting out this window, Matt sees a haze hanging in the downtown sky as if the damaged, disfigured part of the city were being covered with a protective veil. But he knows the World Trade Center is burning; it will burn for weeks and that protective veil is actually a noxious swirl of the products of combustion—asbestos and lead particles, paper turned to ash, human flesh turned to ash . . .

Matt looks away from the window, looks across his hospital bed over at his wife. Ann is still asleep on the cot on the other side of his bed, between the bed and the wall (there is barely space for the cot), and he makes an effort to stop crying. (When did he begin? He has no idea. Since his illness, this happens with some frequency. It is as if he suddenly finds himself walking in two inches of water.) At least Ann is asleep and their fifteen-year-old son is not here to see him cry. Solly has gone to spend the night at a friend's—no one wants to be alone this dreadful night—although Matt cannot remember which friend. Is the medicine burning Matt's mind, throwing a haze over it like the downtown haze so that he cannot remember what anyone tells him, or is Solly retreating from him, not telling him things, is he losing touch with Solly, losing track of his burgeoning boy? He cannot bear that he may not be around to see what that boy will become.

No, Solly has been talking to him, talking double time, Solly talked nonstop today and Matt has forgotten where his son is sleeping because Matt's overloaded. He once said to Ann, forgetting their son was there, "Talk to me. It keeps me alive." And since then Solly has whipped out a constant jumpy stream of talk as though he were a rotary lawn sprinkler and Matt burnt lawn. Which Matt is. But he is being flooded. He has to slow his whirling boy, tell that poor boy he can calm down. Matt is not dying this minute. He imagines putting his hands on Solly's shoulders and turning the boy toward him. But Matt does not have the strength to turn Solly toward him. Solly is only a few inches shorter than Matt now and is gaining weight, and muscle. It is as though there is some private law of thermodynamics at work between them such that no pound is lost in their universe: whatever weight Matt takes off, Solly puts on, and of course Matt is losing weight at an alarming rate. Solly is at an age when he needs a father he can resist, a father he can buck up against, whose bark he can abrade a bit. He does not need a father whose roots are coming loose. Who is standing in water.

The best Matt could do today was wait until Solly left before asking the doctor, how will the blood supply hold out in this catastrophe? The hidden question being, will there be enough blood for me. Matt absorbs great quantities of blood almost daily, especially platelets, that part of the blood that causes clotting. Platelets are oddly not red but straw colored, and Matt puts away pale packet after packet. His body is producing antibodies to the platelets, it is ripping up the platelets and stepping on them, so to speak, even as they are pouring into his veins, which is more than worrisome. But it seems that the city's catastrophe is working in his favor. There were long lines of people waiting hours yesterday to give blood, there were not enough personnel to process all the would-be donors and hook them up to IVs, not enough refrigerators to hold all the blood, the city is awash in blood.

Maybe next time Solly comes, when they go for their walk around the block, Matt will put his hands on his boy's shoulders and simply say Shhhhh. Matt may have to say it through a mask because he is immunosuppressed. (He still feels like an asshole walking outside wearing a pink mask. *That* he hasn't gotten used to.) He wonders suddenly whether the particles in the air at the World Trade Center will diffuse all the way up the nine or ten miles to where he is and further damage his leaky lungs, mask or no. Will he not be able to go out for walks anymore? They are precious to him, those walks with his son. Fuck, he is sick of worrying about himself. Even yesterday, with the city under this wild, weird, unbelievable attack, he feared his doctor would be called away.

Matt also worried because, despite everything, he has to eat. And every time he goes to eat something, he has to think beforehand of the pain he will have (the chemo has left him with sores on the lining of his esophagus and stomach and anus) and is it worth it (yes, he knows he must eat) and can he sit, fold himself up into some position so it will hurt less. This is a three-times-a-day problem and he has come up with various solutions, each of which works a little. For instance, he sits sometimes with both knees under his chin while he eats. He doesn't know why they can't feed him totally through a vein, although they are wary of using up his veins, of destroying them inadvertently, he needs all his veins. Why don't they feed him straight through the catheter into his heart? He must ask his wife. Perhaps she will know.

He turns to look at his sleeping wife, his breathing wife. Ann sleeps facing him. Always facing him. He hardly glances at the TV when she is there (these two days of course have been exceptions), he rarely even looks out the windows, he looks at her. They face each other even in their sleep. Even in separate beds.

He will get back into bed now. Turn toward Ann and, perhaps, fall asleep. Slowly, preparatory to rising, he slides his bottom forward in the chair. Feels a momentary serrated-knife thrust at his tailbone. And a little sensation of breathlessness. He takes a few breaths, pushes down on the wooden arms of the chair and lo! he is standing. Then pulling, half leaning on his pole, he shuffles the one two three steps to the bed and cautiously lets the slippers drop off his feet (do not bend over!), lifts one leg (hands under his thigh), etc. etc., takes a few additional breaths, and he is lying on his side in bed. Facing her.

Lying on her side, she sleeps. (And he didn't wake her! With all his shenanigans!) She wears a green operating-room gown. The white hospital blanket covers her almost to her shoulder, leaving her lovely pink-toned throat visible. She is sleeping quietly, he is happy to see, her mouth relaxed. The lines between her eyebrows are eased, as is the line that starts from each nostril and passes a little wide of the joining of her lips. Despite the nurses coming and going, despite the voices over the intercom, she sleeps best, she says, when she is in the room with him. He teases her that sleeping in the hospital keeps her from raiding the refrigerator during the night; she and Solly are both night feeders—Matt knows they bump into each other in the night kitchen. And in fact she has lost ten pounds since he has become ill. She is happy with herself ten pounds lighter (Matt said, "Every cloud has its slender lining," and they both moaned at the poor pun) and he does suppose that to the world she is more fetching this way, but to him she has always been the dearest thing.

Although sometimes he thinks why him, why not her? He would be devoted.

There is a drop of moisture in the corner of her lip, and he would like to lick it off, work his tongue into her mouth, but besides of course that it would wake her from her few untroubled hours of sleep, he is also afraid to put his tongue into her mouth, his tongue up against her dear tongue, they are both afraid, he is again immunosuppressed: she could kill him. He sees the outline of her breasts through the soft blanket, her heavy breasts, he would like to suck her nipples, it always gave her so much pleasure, but he is afraid, she is afraid. Well, he can touch her nipples with his fingers, *that* he still does. Often he fondles her nipples through her blouse or under her blouse under her bra and she used to leave the hospital barely able to walk, so engorged; he wanted to bring her off with his hand. (A sudden erection he gets now, well, at least that is not wholly suppressed.) But she was afraid. Suppose, she said, suppose he has a cut, a microscopic cut on a finger, and then some bacteria from her vaginal juices would enter in . . .

Well, he said one day, suppose he wears those latex gloves, the really thin ones, the ones surgeons wear. She shivered, fearing it, wanting it, he supposed.

"I'll double-glove," he said finally.

And so he triple-gloved and they both wore masks, and she wore a paper gown over her clothes, and paper hospital booties, and her luxurious hair was caught up in a paper hairnet and for humor's sake and symmetry he caught up his no-hair in a paper hairnet. What they must look like, this pair, to the world (of the well)! But the world was barricaded out. Up against the door she set not only one of the chairs but the garbage pail and his tray table. They stood next to each other for a moment grinning into the bathroom mirror, "like two ani-mated condoms," he said, and she hooted.

In bed she placed a little disposable plastic chuck beneath her and slipped down her pants. Sitting up next to her, he opened her labia with sheathed fingers, touched her sweet clitoris, massaged it gently, and his hands trembled, and Ann trembled (they were both full of fear and trembling) and Ann came very fast. And he wept. Because she came and because it was over so fast and they were back to themselves with her underpants down around her ankles, the pad beneath her, and leukemia.

"What can I do for *you?*" she asked, seeing his erection through his loose hospital pants.

Next day he spoke (man to man) to Dr. Mears. Mears wasn't sure—had no one ever asked him, not ever? He told Matt, "Nothing should happen." The doctor nodded, smiled, murmured, "Give it a shot." But their gambling impulse was gone and they ended up making love only during the weeks Matt wasn't immunosuppressed, the weeks he was home.

But one time when they barricaded the door, she stood in the middle of the small room and slowly, shyly, unbuttoned her blouse. *Please*, he said, his voice tremulous, and he moved out of bed carefully (not just because he was ill but also because he had an erection) to sit in the chair and watch. And she wriggled out of the blouse and gave it a little toss onto the bold tray table and unhooked her black bra. Brown-nippled breasts fell out, still a little heavy, a little bulky (it was his Ann). She unzipped, then stepped out of her skirt, and her slip, so she was in just a pair of old black panties—you could see the elastic around the legs coming through the black cotton, they'd been washed so many times. She stepped out of them, too, so he could see her (still) glorious bushy bush, his hair was so sparse everywhere. And she was a thick bushy loamy forest to him. And her (a little wrinkled) thighs rolled beneath and to the sides of the forest as she swayed in the middle of the small room. She turned her puckered wondrous tush toward him, swung it back and forth, turned round a few times. And she sang a little Shakespeare for him, before him, sang low softly *with a hey nonny ho nonny ho* as he sat in the chair with the wooden arms like a king.

Three

Matt makes it into the first 40 percent, those who go into remission from the chemotherapy.

When he comes home from the hospital, Ann gives herself a two-week vacation from work. The sight, however scrawny, and the (nonmedicinal) smell of Matt thrill her, and she is always following him, touching him. If he is shaving, she gets a kick out of sitting on the toilet seat and watching; or if he is showering, she hops in with him even if she just showered—at the least, she brings him towels she's warmed up in the dryer.

After his long, austere stay in the hospital, Matt responds to her shadowing and pampering him with bursts of physical affection so intense that Solly threatens to run away from home. And he grumbles about the childish horseplay his parents are suddenly into—his mother's throwing a blanket over his father's legs may lead to a tug-of-war, or her plumping his pillows, a fight that leaves the living room a feathery mess.

One day Solly comes home early from rehearsal and hears his mother laughing flirtatiously as his father belts out childish songs in their bedroom: "Oh, what does a Scotsman wear under his kilt? A shlong! A shlong!

"Do your balls hang low? Do they wobble to and fro? Can you tie them in a knot? Can you tie them in a bow?"

"For Christ sake!" Solly yells as he takes off with his homework for a pizza place.

Matt gains back six (and more coming) of the twenty pounds he lost and grows a stubbly field of dark, peppery hair. His skin returns to flesh tone. His blue eyes, which had grown watery, blue again.

Despite the cold weather, he cannot stay in the house but must be walking outside forever. To walk unnoticed delights him. "With that mask on, I felt like a mangy dog with a fluorescent muzzle."

Several times he comes home from his outings with a

plant or an armload of fresh flowers, mortal dangers to the
immunosuppressed, which he, thankfully, no longer is. He
also brings back germy things from the supermarket—
raw vegetables and fruits with the skin on—which he eats
with relish. He frequents lectures, movies, restaurants, parent–
teacher meetings—anywhere where there are crowds of
people and, especially, small children, some of whom presum-
ably have colds.

Each day Matt stays healthy is a day fewer of the one thousand eight hundred and twenty-five days—the five years—
he needs to survive so he can be considered cured. Ann
marks it off on the calendar first thing in the morning and
then checks the Internet to find out is there any new research
on acute myelogenous leukemia, what does the National
Institutes of Health have to say, what does Medline, are there
any new drugs on the horizon since she went to sleep? Matt
tells her to forget about it, that is Dr. Mears's job, and while
Matt appreciates her concern, he is determined not to dimin-
ish his life by focusing on its finiteness. "All of our lives are
finite."

Two weeks into the new semester—Matt has returned to teaching in January—Ann points out a black-and-blue mark on
his forehead. "I probably banged myself," he says, "although I
don't remember it." When it is still there at the end of the week,
she suggests he go to the dermatologist, who tells him, "You
mustn't be so careless." A second black-and-blue mark appears
on the day of his monthly appointment with Dr. Mears.

"I'm coming with you," Ann says.

Matt shakes his head.

"Why not?"

"Don't make a big production out of everything. If there's a problem, I'll phone you."

Ann feels she shouldn't insist.

She calls from the Metropolitan Museum, where she has just seen a Vermeer show with two women friends, art historians. "How'd the appointment go?"

"Fine, dear."

"Really?"

"Yes. Mears says I'm fine."

"What did he make of those things on your forehead?"

"Nothing! He didn't know what they were."

"He didn't know what they were?"

"Nope. No idea."

"Did you show them to him?"

"He couldn't exactly miss them."

"You asked him, though, and he said he didn't know what they were."

"That's right. Enjoy dinner with your friends—give Lisa a hug from me."

"You're sure you don't mind?"

"Not at all."

"And you're fine. You're absolutely fine?"

"Absolutely."

She arrives home a little tipsy, wearing the new pair of silvery pearl earrings she'd bought at the museum after she spoke to Matt. They are a copy of the earring worn by the sitter in *Girl with a Pearl Earring*. Even though that model was probably thirty-five years younger than Ann, and Ann has never modeled for anyone, and there are five centuries between them—she feels, with her husband healthy before her, more elated, and even more beautiful, than that soulful immortal girl. Standing in the living room with her coat still on, she does a slow three-hundred-sixty-degree turn in front of Matt, who watches rapt from the sofa. The earrings give off a warm human light.

Then he stands up and helps her out of her coat and takes her in his arms. "I've never lied to you before in our marriage, but these—these"—he points at the black-and-blue marks on his forehead—"these damned spots are 'chloromas,' I think Mears called them. They're—accumulations of—blast cells— under the skin." He sighs.

"No." Ann lifts her hands to his face and slowly caresses his chin and his nose and his cheeks but not his forehead. Her hands tremble so that he has to hold them down; he stands there in the living room pressing her hands against his face.

And then Solly comes home and they tell him.

"Fuck this shit," he yells as he runs back out of the house.

At two in the morning Matt and Ann go to bed. Matt wants to make love and he asks her to put on the earrings. "You looked so happy when you walked in wearing them."

Ann puts them on, but very soon they seem to irritate her earlobes and she has difficulty concentrating and can't come no matter what Matt does or she does. Finally she takes the earrings off and still can't come.

Well, what does she expect?

When he seems to be asleep, she goes into the bathroom

where she can see in the mirror that her right earlobe is almost as red as her eyes.

Late that night—she never falls asleep—Ann scoops the earrings off her bedside table and goes to the window and opens it. A cold burst of air hits her. She throws the earrings out into the night as far as she can.

Four

In the air-conditioned hospital room Matt and Ann sit on his bed, looking up expectantly at the little bag of his brother's bone marrow cells that hangs from the metal IV pole. Elaine, the nurse, stands beside the bed smiling; she is tall and fair-skinned, her blond hair twined into a single braid. Hugging the ceiling is a bunch of silver HAPPY BIRTHDAY balloons, their long waving stems tied together with a glossy blue ribbon. Each balloon reads IT'S A BOY! as does the blue banner on the wall over Matt's bed. The nurses make these festivities a part of every transplant, which is, after all, a chance at a new life.

It is a little like having the waiters at a restaurant sing "Happy Birthday," Ann thinks. She likes it when they sing for her, but at the same time she feels foolish for feeling gratified. Her husband does not get a kick out of folderol, not for himself, anyway, but she knows he wouldn't hurt Elaine's feelings. After all, the nurse has been looking after him for months now—ever since he arrived at the Fred Hutchinson Cancer Research Center in Seattle—so she is almost part of the family.

Matt, pale, reaches over and pats Ann's hands. Trying to keep her spirits up. She imagines he would like to pat that little bag of cells, wish his remaining strength, wish all of their strength, Elaine's, Ann's, *everybody's* (maybe not their son's) into those fresh brave red bodies and bid them Godspeed if he believed in God.

No. He does everything he can to stay alive—he is an earnest patient—but he would not leech the world. Not even in fantasy.

She would. (Although she wouldn't touch their son.) Or she would curse God and die.

Ann is a believer, even if lately mostly in the malevolence of the universe. She prays fervently now, silently reciting each Hebrew blessing she remembers from childhood, the blessing over bread and the blessing over wine, the three Hanukah prayers that are sung over the candles (she sings them in her mind), the Shema Yisrael, also "May you go from strength to strength," and "Thank you, Lord, for keeping me alive to see this day." She is not so sure about the last. She thinks it is meant for joyous occasions. Well, let this be a joyous occasion.

With the ease of much practice, Elaine turns the stopcock. The dark-red cells begin to drip slowly down the clear tubular plastic wire, they aggregate and fill up the tube, it becomes a red tube that makes its way under Matt's pajamas and disappears into his chest. Elaine smoothes any crimps out of the line, more as a ceremonial gesture than a necessity.

Despite the bombardment of experimental treatments— during the past months, the doctors at this world-famous Seattle blood cancer center have thrown every cockamamie protocol at him, every outré treatment known on earth for his condition—Matt's disease has not budged, or not much. It has not "remitted," as they say.

Every bone marrow transplant is complicated, Ann knows by now. Children under the age of six do well. The children's wing of the hospital is full of these little bald lucky ones, their faces swollen with steroids, the violet veins showing through their fragile bluish scalps.

For most other patients, a bone marrow transplant is what the doctors among themselves call a "heroic measure" or a "hope to Jesus" play; they are right up there, bone marrow transplants, with exenterations and hemipelvectomies. But the doctors do not tell that to the insurance companies nor do they tell the patients, not in so many words.

Ann, of course, knows enough, even as a psychiatrist, to appreciate the oncologists' skepticism. But she does not mention it to her husband. Nor to their son, when he comes to visit. She has grown inward about many things.

For instance, the results of the spinal tap indicate that Matt now has leukemic cells in his spinal fluid. It does not make his chances of survival any worse, they are already worse, but she has told the doctors not to tell him unless he asks. He has not asked.

When they found out the doctors were going to do the transplant without getting Matt into remission, Ann wept in the bathroom. Matt knocked on the door and when she came out fast thinking maybe he needed to use the toilet, he put his arms around her and touched her tearstained face and said, "It's not over yet."

She now cries only in bathrooms on other floors, and she tries not to cry ever in front of him or their son—or in front of anybody, not even in the support groups for relatives. She attends those once or twice a week with other wives or husbands of patients, also parents of children and teenagers. Members disappear and new ones appear at a frightening rate. At each meeting people "share": fellow church members at far-away parishes are holding cookouts and raffles and sending the proceeds to help cover the cost of the transplant—enormous, for those who have no insurance; some television, computer, and Internet hookups are better than others to keep in touch with "loved ones" back home; nausea and vomiting can be controlled occasionally by (cooked) ground root of ginger, obtainable at Susie Chin's, a naturopathy store at 21 Pound Street. Earlier in Matt's illness she had cried easily, "healthily." Now she is worried she might start a panic. Everyone would stampede for the doors.

So she does not cry at these support groups any longer but instead she often loses something, once her wallet, another time a ring, a third time her "to do" list. Each time, she returns to the small hospital room where the groups are held (it is an inside windowless off-white room with posters of paintings from the local Frye Art Museum—a painting of Amsterdam, and of an old man sitting in the sunlight) and lifts the stiff pillows off the buttercup-yellow sofa and matching chairs. She gets down on all fours to search beneath the furniture (the dust down there does not inspire confidence); shakes out the few books and magazines. Always, she finds whatever it is she lost, and each recovery occasions a few hours' celebratory feeling. She has started wondering whether she is losing things on purpose in order to find them.

The little cells take no more than twenty minutes to vanish altogether, whereupon the nurse removes the line and caps Matt's catheter, and brings out two small chocolate birthday cupcakes with MATT handwritten on one in blue icing, MA on the other. Elaine hands the second cupcake to Ann, who thinks perhaps the TT fell off, or the kitchen ran out of icing. Or— and here comes a bizarre idea—perhaps the baker knows, God forbid, that soon Ann may no longer be a wife, she will be only a mother. The cupcakes have no milk in them; for some reason Matt is not allowed milk. Ann thinks about not eating her cupcake because she does not want to be only a mother, but in the end she devours it. Matt washes his hands with soapless soap that he releases from a container attached to the wall beside his bed, then opens the cellophane wrapper around his fork and knife, and cuts out a couple of bite-size pieces from the sides of his cupcake. Ann wonders if he is avoiding cutting through his name.

"Delicious." He beams at the nurse.

And Ann does not say, But you hardly ate any. She simply nods and smiles in agreement.

Matt is warned he will grow weaker (although Ann cannot imagine how he could grow any weaker), and over the next few days he *does* grow weaker as the new cells engraft. It is crucial that they engraft. The chemo and radiation have destroyed, the doctors hope, most of his capacity to make new cells—he was making mostly leukemic cells. His brother's cells, which have been "transplanted," must move in and take up residence and begin producing new, healthy cells. And they do seem to have moved in! By the end of the first week, his graft is sending out new immature red cells, and new immature white cells! But also it is sending out immune cells against Matt's own body; the graft is recognizing Matt's body as "foreign," as an enemy, and is launching an attack. A little attack, a little graft-versus-host disease, is a good thing; it means the new bone marrow is in there and functioning. Already the graft has attacked his gut and his skin. And so he has sores on his tongue, which make it difficult to speak; he experiences a ripping sensation upon eliminating; he tries not to scratch at the rosy itchy rash that covers his back and chest. The gastroenterologist has visited him, and the dermatologist has visited him, and each has administered new medicines, which help some. And every day his blood is drawn and the hematologist renders his report, while Matt and Ann listen with the terrified attention Moses must have given to God thundering down the Ten Commandments.

Because Matt is speaking little and forcing himself to eat, the doctors are worried he is depressed. Ann assures them he is only normally—"situationally"—depressed. They send a psychiatrist anyway, who asks Matt who the president is and can Matt subtract seven from a hundred and keep subtracting seven. He can but it hurts his tongue. What would Matt want if he could have three wishes?

"To eat. To have my gut not hurt. To survive."

The psychiatrist offers to prescribe an antidepressant although he agrees Matt is not clinically depressed. Matt thanks him for his wish to do something, but declines.

Matt shows Ann a full-page Alvin Ailey Company ad in the *Seattle Times* ("Oh, how fine they do dance!") and so she knows, before Matt tells her, that Lucinda Wylie, a principal Ailey dancer, will be stopping by. Ann smiles fiercely. Lucinda and Matt had an affair many years ago, before he met

Ann. Through Lucinda's two marriages, the first to a wealthy
Swede, the second to a black writer, Lucinda has kept in touch.
Matt's relationship with her has always worried Ann, although
she believes, and Matt has reassured her, that her worries are
groundless. Since Lucinda and Matt see each other not that
much, maybe once a year that Ann is aware of, Ann worries
not that much. Still, now, Ann takes shallow breaths through
her mouth for a few moments until she can breathe normally.
The next day, she notes with some small satisfaction that her
last thought on falling asleep as well as her earliest thought on
awakening this morning—neither thought had anything to do
with Lucinda.

Ann sees her first. She is striding down the hospital hallway
in a form-fitting vermilion dress, which flares at the thighs.
Crystal drop earrings swinging as she walks, Lucinda wears
her straightened hair in a taut upsweep high on her head. She
is at least seven feet tall, Ann thinks, the healthiest person
Ann has ever seen. In her presence the patients plodding the
hallway seem to be lifting their feet a little higher, a nurse
pushes her pill cart with more vigor. Lucinda takes both of
Ann's hands and says deeply, "How *is* he? How *are* you?" Her
hazel eyes burn in her dark face.

Ann looks up at her, mumbles, "Okay. All right," and in
trying to get her voice to normal volume, hears herself howling. Lucinda embraces her. Ann is ashamed that the fucking
tears start. After a while Lucinda reaches into her pocketbook
and offers a package of tissues to Ann who shakes her head
and points at the big box of tissues on the supply table behind
them in the hallway. When she has control of her voice (it
sounds robotic to her ears), she thanks Lucinda for coming.

Lucinda grimaces and, with long fingers, waves away Ann's thanks.

Ann explains the dress code, opening the drawer of the night table to hand Lucinda a mask and gloves and an extra-large paper gown. Lucinda nods confusedly and gets into the outfit, which somehow looks stylish on her, raffish. Ann dresses also, feeling small and dowdy, and the two enter Matt's room.

He is dozing, snoring lightly, and when Lucinda looks at him, her forehead gullies and her bright eyes darken and she seems to lose a few inches in stature. She sways for a moment so that Ann wonders if she is praying, and then realizes she is possibly crumpling at the knees. Ann should bring her a chair. But Ann is overwhelmed by seeing in Lucinda's face and body how ill Matt is.

Matt wakes glumly, sees Ann and brightens, sees Lucinda and brightens—more? Yes, more. Oh, who can measure degrees, shades of brightening? And isn't Ann delighted to see Matt brighten? Ann breathes slowly and tells herself that Matt has not seen Lucinda in a year, not since he's been ill, while he saw Ann just before he took his nap.

Matt says to Lucinda, "I wish I could hug you. I wish I could kiss you."

Ann wants to kick him, but it occurs to her with the force of revelation, that he would not say such things in front of her if she had anything, had ever had anything to fear.

Lucinda sits down and Matt takes her hands in his and after a long moment of looking at each other, the two begin to talk.

Mumbling something about old friends needing privacy, Ann leaves the room almost on tiptoe. Perhaps Matt says, "Bye, dear." Or perhaps he is calling Lucinda "my dear." Ann is not sure. She does not turn back.

Pain. And anger at herself for feeling the pain, the same old pain, whether warranted or not. So she still has energy for jealousy, that waste of emotion, that green-eyed monster. No, Lucinda is the green-eyed monster. Still there, Lucinda is.

One gets over nothing in this life.

Ann sheds her paper outfit into the special metal receptacle outside Matt's door, and walks down the hallway, down the elevator, through another hallway and then the lobby and finally out into the world.

The sun is shining and she closes her eyes and lifts her face to it. She is glad to be outside. In natural light and heat. Much heat. She begins to walk briskly down Marion Street, feeling her muscles move, liking the feeling. Lucinda is not the only one with muscles. Ann walks fast, faster, taking some enjoyment in feeling the skin of her forehead, of her neck, moisten. She is nearly running over the busy underpass that is Interstate 5; she turns down Pike Street and then she is really running. Past a diner, a Starbucks, a Gap, she is flying. She feels lighter despite sweat dripping down her face, her blouse sticking against her shoulders. In the distance she sees the bright blue water of Elliott Bay—she would like to run on the sand along the bay—but she is slowed by crowds of tourists just outside Pike Place Market, a covered two-story farmer's market-cum-tourist attraction. She entered it once before with their son, remembers masses of bright flowers and vegetables; an odd fish-tossing ritual at the "flying fish market"; and, of all things, a shoe museum—SHOES OF MYSTERY and SEE A SHOE

ACTUALLY WORN BY WORLD'S TALLEST MAN. Also a store that specializes in condoms; in the window there was a basket labeled THE WORLD'S BEST SELECTION—YOU BE THE JUDGE. Her son had looked impish and seemed to avoid her eyes, and she hoped that meant he had something to hide, that their family disaster had not gotten totally in the way of his teenage years.

She enters the market, admires display crates of cherries—Queen Anne's cherries (she wishes she could bring some back for Matt, but he can't even have them in the room, let alone eat them), purple-black Bing cherries, Rainier cherries. Next to them are boxes of peaches—O'Henrys, Risingstars; and Washington State apples—Fujis, Pink Ladies ... After the harsh white-and-chrome geometry of the hospital, she revels in the vibrant colors, the soft roundnesses, the silly names. She chooses an assortment of fruit for herself, and asks the produce seller to wash them. It is Seattle, and so he nods and lifts up a hose and sprays away. She eats a few wet cherries, spitting the pits on the floor, takes a bite of a Cresthaven peach, lets the juices run down her chin.

She stands before the famous fish market, a sign overhead reading CAUTION: LOW-FLYING FISH. There are crates of slimy white tubular squid. Packed on ice are banks of fish, shoals of king salmon next to rows of black cod and bluefish and spotted trout, species after species; there are overlapping layers of golden crabs, their eyes open at the viewer, behind them the sign OUR DUNGENESS CRABS ARE SO FRESH YOU NEED A VIDEO CAMERA TO FILM THEM.

She watches a woman in her early fifties with a camera round her neck cry out, "Three pounds of salmon!" Beside the woman stand her husband and prepubertal son, who has a look of disgust on his face. A fishmonger in a whitish apron selects a salmon; the eyes are black flattened discs bordered by golden rings, which are cracked now, no longer perfectly round. The man waves the salmon at the buyer, who nods and snaps photos, her flash lighting again and again. He flings the chosen fish at the next fellow down the line, who catches and lays the fish down and guts it, then throws the open fish at the next man in a wet, pale-pink-splashed apron (all the men on the line wear spattered chef's aprons) who hacks off the head—Ann winces—and, dropping the dripping cleaver neatly, weighs the salmon and cries out its price. After the woman has set down the money, he throws the remains of the fish to the last fellow on the line who wraps it in brown paper and ties it with string and hands it to the startled son while his mother is snapping and flashing away.

The sweat on Ann's body has cooled off and she is uncomfortably chilly, actually shivering.

Five

In the Seattle apartment Ann is on her hands and knees cleaning the kitchen floor with a mixture of bleach and disinfectant when the phone rings. She has already wiped down the sink and counters and cleaned the bathroom. Every other day for the past three weeks, ever since Matt was released from the hospital at the beginning of August, she has washed the floor and the counters. Also she has been scrubbing all fruits and vegetables before cooking them, boiling drinking glasses, fumigating for pests . . . Beneath the purple rubber gloves, her fingertips are white and wrinkled. Maybe she needs a new pair of gloves. Or maybe the rubber irritates her skin.

Although it is eleven in the morning and the phone is ringing, Solly is still asleep in the second bedroom. He arrived late last night from New York and they ate grilled-cheese sandwiches and watched some television and went to bed. But Ann thinks she heard him in the living room during the night and she knows he was on the phone at six in the morning because when she began to dial in to check messages, she heard him talking to a girl. Is it a girlfriend, Ann wonders, and hopes.

The phone continues ringing and she knows she will not be able to get to it before the automated service picks up. She is in the final corner and it takes her only a few minutes before she removes her gloves and punches in the number and password. The new message is from Elaine (Ann thinks of her as "their" nurse), and it is a request that Matt call as soon as he can.

This is odd. Generally on the days Matt is not at the hospital, Elaine phones in his blood results from the previous day and closes with a cheery "Say Hi to Ann. See you tomorrow." Occasionally she will add that she needs to talk to him about something in particular—once, his catheter, and another time, his medications—but she always says what it is. Maybe today she is rushed. Ann washes her hands, rubs down the phone with a medicinal wipe, and walks to the balcony and hands the phone to Matt.

In the bright sunlight he punches in the nurse's number, which he knows by heart, punches in the special code, which gets him onto her private line, and says, "Hi there, Elaine. It's Matt here. What's the good word?" Ann watches as he listens, watches as his forehead scrunches up. "You want to see us both?" he asks. "What's up?" She watches as he closes his eyes. Then he says quietly, "Okay. Yes. We'll be there." He stands for a moment with the phone at his ear. The sunlight is so bright behind him she thinks that is the reason he has closed his eyes. But it is she who is looking into the sunlight and his image is going black.

Matt walks into the living room, closes the balcony door, pulls the Venetian blind.

Her eyes have not yet adjusted, so she cannot see his face as he says, "There's something wrong with the test results. They're running them again through some special machine at University Hospital. Elaine wants us to meet the whole team at the clinic at four o'clock."

In the dark Ann reaches for the phone.

"No," he says. "They won't know for sure until four."

He puts his arms around her. They hold each other tight.

"Keep busy," he says. "It may be nothing."

She nods. Slowly she collects all the different wastebaskets and empties them into the kitchen garbage can and knots the full plastic bag and takes it out to the garbage room. She starts vacuuming. Then she remembers Solly is sleeping. She makes their bed. She gets the stack of bills and sits at the living-room computer entering them. Matt walks in, picks up this article, that manila envelope, touches her neck, goes back out onto the balcony. She nearly cries out. She prints the checks, signs them, places them in envelopes. After she seals the envelopes, she opens them to make sure she has put each check in the right envelope. Matt walks in again, touches her shoulder, kisses the tip of her ear. She worries for a moment but then remembers she showered last night, she washed her hair in the shower this morning. She gets into the shower and washes her hair again. Rubs off some of the dead, wrinkled skin from the tips of her fingers. Stops herself from rubbing off more. After she has dried off and is in the bedroom putting on fresh clothes, she can hear Solly is up. It is two o'clock.

When she goes into the living room, Matt is on the balcony telling Solly about the meeting. Their son is squinting, not only his eyes but also his nose and mouth. "Of course, I'm coming," he grunts. He picks up a basketball from somewhere, from thin air, and dribbles it through the living room and out of the apartment.

At three thirty Solly is back and they set out in the still-bright sunlight, Ann with a yellow pad and pencil. She holds Matt's cold hand. Solly is dribbling the ball a little in front of them, wearing a sweaty black T-shirt that says on the back in small white letters, IF YOU CAN READ THIS, YOU'RE TOO CLOSE. Even hunched over the ball he is still a little taller than Matt, and he has bulked up. Nowadays when Solly is with them, she often sees him doing push-ups and squats. Maybe that was what he was doing in the living room in the middle of the night.

At the clinic Matt and Ann usually schmooze with other families in the large waiting area until the technician is ready to take blood or the doctor is ready to examine Matt. Today, the receptionist immediately ushers them out of the waiting area and leaves them in an empty conference room. It is a few minutes before four. The large wooden table is the largest they've seen and there are too many chairs. Ann and Matt sit next to each other. The basketball in his lap, Solly sits near the door, leaving two empty chairs between him and them. Ann makes aimless marks on the yellow pad. Matt rises and paces by the window. The chairs are on rollers, and Solly rolls back and forth noisily along the wall adjacent to the door. Matt asks Solly to recite for him, to recite anything at all. After a while, Solly stops moving and begins:

On the ground
Sleep sound:
I'll apply
To your eye . . .

But his voice is lumpy, and he falters and breaks off. He returns to rolling. Ann knows the rest of the passage—it is a favorite of Matt's, from *A Midsummer Night's Dream*—but no one has the heart to recite it.

Finally, at four thirty the team enters, walking close together. Dr. Kris Doney, who is wearing a white sweater over her pink summery dress (a few flowers peep out through the loose mesh of the sweater), shakes their hands as do Dr. Alex Reubs and Alice Cort, the social worker. The nurse, Elaine, holds Matt's thick folder in her large hands. She puts the folder down on the table and shakes both Matt's hands and then both of Ann's and nods vigorously at Solly.

The members of the team seat themselves beside each other at the head of the table. They are a long distance away. Kris Doney speaks. "You are undoubtedly wondering why we called this meeting. Well, I am sorry to have to tell you that there were quite a few misshapen cells in yesterday's blood sample, a run of them, really, and we were hoping that they would turn out to be immature cells, that the graft was putting out new cells too soon. We did the usual tests on them and then, to be absolutely sure, we sent the sample out to University Hospital, where they have a very sensitive state-of-the-art spectro—" Kris Doney pauses and Ann almost jumps in to ask what kind of machine she is talking about. Why doesn't Dr. Doney say the whole word, tell the name of it? Maybe Ann has run across the machine during her medical school training. No, that wouldn't be likely if it's state of the art . . . Ann shakes her head at herself and keeps quiet. Kris Doney shakes her head, too, several times. "I'm sorry to have to tell you," she says. "but it's—unfortunately, very unfortunately, the leukemia—well, it's back."

Solly rises from his chair, lifts the basketball up over his head with both hands, and sends it crashing through the wall-size window.

Everyone recoils and the social worker's small hands jerk up protectively in front of her face. One big jagged piece of glass lands intact in the middle of the conference table, many slivers shower down on the floor, and three small, lacy-edged bits of glass, all that is left of the window, remain stuck, almost decorously, in one side of the still-shuddering frame. Most of the glass has crashed down outside, although no horns honk, no one cries out for help. The sky is very large and blue.

Suddenly Matt, who is hugging himself, laughs. He stops for a moment, takes a deep breath, and then really bursts out. He is guffawing. Sitting next to him, watching him at first in astonishment, Ann begins to chuckle haltingly and then gives way to a high-pitched cackle. Elaine smiles at the two of them, then giggles, then laughs heartily from her belly. Soon her big body is bouncing in her seat, her braid has come half loose and is swinging back and forth with her heaving bosom. The others join in, chortling and tinkling, the little social worker is doubled over. It is like the breaking of a summer storm in hideously humid weather and no one much minds getting soaked to the skin just so long as the weather changes.

Ann says between hoots, "What do we do now?"

Everyone calms down except for Solly, who has never joined the laughter, and Matt. No one wants to interrupt Matt laughing. Matt is actually roaring. It is difficult to tell if he is beside himself with mirth or rage. After a while, he wipes his face with a handkerchief and grins. "My kid's got quite an arm there, don't you think? A real David with a slingshot."

Solly, still standing, although his arms are down at his sides, shoots his father a dark look.

"Of course, we'll pay for the window." Matt is still smiling although he has grown quiet.

"Butt out," Solly growls. "It's my fucking window."

Alex Reubs says hastily, "The window belongs to the Hutch. Fred Hutchinson Cancer Research Center. Insurance. Sports accident. Act of God."

The room is quite warm now despite the overworking air conditioner. Alex Reubs is loosening his tie and there are sweat stains at the armpits of Elaine's green shirt. The nurse goes out and returns with a pitcher of ice water and paper cups. She fills the cups and passes them around without looking at anyone. Everyone drinks greedily.

When they have finished—Matt drinks three glasses of water as though what is wrong with him is dehydration—Kris Doney says gently, "You folks can return to New York whenever you want."

Six

In New York, Ann has the feeling the apartment has been rearranged. Maybe it is just that there is a lot of stuff around, the stuff of their lives, there has always been a lot of stuff around, she is not good at throwing things out, the place is heavy, thick, she can't find things. She can't breathe. Ann misses the bareness, the newness, of the small Seattle apartment—the hopefulness.

Twice a week Matt goes to Dr. Mears's office for a blood transfusion, and a hospice nurse comes round to the apartment every few days. She leaves a big DO NOT RESUSCITATE sign, which they tape up on the wall over their bed.

Finally Matt is bedridden. Ann does not understand how he will get his blood transfusions if he is too weak to take a cab to Dr. Mears's office. She calls to find out will they send over a technician. She is put on hold. Dr. Mears gets on the phone. "Ann, are you alone? Take the phone into another room."

"Why? I'm in the bedroom with Matt."

"Please."

She walks down the hall, which is lined with their wedding photographs, to Matt's small office.

"Is the door closed?" Dr. Mears asks.

"I don't see why there's anything you can't tell me in Matt's presence." There is a photo of her on Matt's desk in a white nightgown holding two-day-old naked Solly. He is reddish and pudgy with large testicles. On the wall hangs a sculpture of Chekhov's delicate bearded face.

"Ann, sit down. Try to pay attention."

"Of course I'm paying attention."

"If you bring Matt here to get a transfusion, I'll have to keep him in the hospital—he's that sick. He wants to die at home. Ann, he's going to die. In the next few days."

"I'm not talking about bringing Matt over to *you*. That's out of the question. Why can't you send someone *here* to give him a transfusion, *that's* what I'm asking. It'll buy him more time—"

"Ann, listen to me. With or without a transfusion he's going to die in the next few days. His blood is full of leukemic cells. I can't clear them anymore."

"You're going to just leave him like that?"

"Ann, you're in denial."

"What? What are you talking about?"

"He's going to die, Ann. Any day now."

She hangs up on him. She feels stunned and queasy, as if Dr. Mears has stopped being Matt's doctor, as if he has just whispered some drunken obscene suggestion in her ear. She considers calling another oncologist. She phones the hospice nurse, but leaves no message. In Matt's office Ann sits at his desk running her fingers over his computer keyboard without hitting any of the keys.

When she walks into their bedroom, Solly is reciting some Shakespeare for Matt.

Sitting up in bed, Matt applauds. "More," he says. And Solly recites more.

Ann takes off her shoes and sits down on the bed and listens to their son run his Shakespearean marathon. At eleven o'clock Matt applauds for the last time.

Ann is kicked awake at three in the morning, kicked almost out of bed. But she manages to hold on to the bedpost and so finds herself sitting in the upper corner of the bed, nearly on top of her pillow. She turns the light on and sees that Matt has moved into a diagonal position. His head is at the far upper corner of the bed, but his legs must have swept across and pushed her, his torso is in the middle of the bed, his feet are now on her side of the bed. "What is it, dear?" she asks, from her sitting position. He doesn't answer. "Are you uncomfortable?" Again he doesn't answer. She massages her right hip for a moment, for that is where he kicked her—probably he kneed her. When she tries to push him back to his side of the bed, he doesn't budge. "Matt!"

He answers something unintelligible about sharks.

She turns the light toward him.

His eyes are open but he seems not to recognize her.

She holds him. He tries to speak, but moans. And keeps moaning.

"Are you in pain, dear?"

He can only moan. It is hard for him to catch his breath. She sees the way the spaces between his ribs suck in mightily each time he breathes. She thinks to call Dr. Mears. But she remembers his "you're in denial" and anyway it is the middle of the night. She could call 911, but what will the police do? If they come, they will take Matt away. Should she wake Solly? She feels for Matt's pulse and has trouble finding it. It is slight and slow, she counts forty beats one minute, thirty the next. After listening to Matt moaning and fighting to breathe for five minutes and watching his position in bed—he remains unmoving, rigid—she goes slowly (her hip still smarts) into the kitchen and takes from the refrigerator one of the morphine suppositories the hospice nurse has left her. She dons a rubber glove, applies ointment, and then with her free hand presses against Matt's shoulder as hard as she can and so manages to tilt him a little onto his side. With difficulty, she inserts the suppository into his rectum.

She kisses his dry lips. She brings a damp washcloth and soothes his lips. She holds a few ice chips between her fingers to his tongue. He moans less, and so she feels she has done something for him, and every few hours she brings him another suppository. She kisses him from his forehead to his diaper to his bony toes.

By the next evening he is dead.

Seven

Matt is running through the corridors of the hospital in Seattle wielding a white plastic knife, threatening to kill everyone. It is the kind of disposable knife people use at picnics. Three policemen restrain him with great difficulty. So all this time he has been diagnosed incorrectly! They have been treating him for cancer when clearly he is suffering from paranoid schizophrenia, a terrible illness. They must call a psychiatric consult immediately and start prescribing the proper medications. Ann wakes unutterably—oh so briefly—happy.

At the packed funeral, many people speak, some at length: his publisher, his agent, the chair of his department, his brother . . . It is hard for her to pay attention—she keeps waiting for Matt to get up and speak for himself. He will be brief and humorous. She does hear the rabbi say that while Matt was not a believer, *he*, the rabbi, is a believer, and he calls upon God to account for the crime of Matt's early death.

Outside, waiting for the limousine to the graveyard, she and Solly are thronged. Everyone seems to want to touch them as if they are, for the moment, anointed. In a long black dress, Lucinda Wylie sweeps through the crowd (does she walk *above* the crowd? No, not now that Matt is dead), her hair rolled into a dark chignon studded with jet beads, her arms ringed with large ebony and silver bracelets. Lucinda takes both of Ann's hands, and the ebony and silver bracelets make musical sounds as they knock against each other—a wooden clacker, a triangle.

A young woman with blue eyes and bright-brown hair in a simple brown sweater and skirt comes over and Solly introduces her to his mother as Gina Pappadopolis, Stuy graduate, freshman at Yale. Gina takes Ann's hand gravely. Solly introduces his mother to Gina's parents, a heavyset grim-looking man in an olive suit and a blue-eyed woman in a gray dress who carries a black patent-leather pocketbook. There is a carefulness in the way Solly pronounces their names and brings their hands to Ann's. He stands up very straight and even his gold earring seems subdued and respectful, almost antique.

At the cemetery the rabbi intones in Hebrew and then in English that the Lord is great and good and that His name is sanctified forever throughout the world, which He has created according to His will. Everyone present throws some dirt down onto the coffin. Solly shovels and shovels and fills up the rest of the grave himself while everyone waits, although it takes Solly close to half an hour and the rabbi looks angry and Solly gets a blister on the palm of his hand; his uncle Adam ties his handkerchief around Solly's torn skin.

Among the condolence letters is an autopsy report. Do families routinely receive a copy? Perhaps it arrives because she is a physician.

The body is that of a cachectic male with alopecia, with multiple petechiae over his abdomen, bilateral thighs . . . Stomach: Reveals multiple ulcerated areas with pale centers rimmed in dark red . . . Kidneys: Right and left appear pale, with multiple hemorrhagic foci . . . Examination of the abdomen: Reveals 2,750 ml of serous peritoneal fluid.

She quits reading and considers ripping up the report, but cannot bear to throw away anything having to do with Matt.

Leaving her office one day at dusk, she sees Matt walking home ahead of her. He has that spring in his step—she quickens her step to catch up with him—and he is carrying his worn brown-leather briefcase stuffed with papers and he is wearing that new suit, the navy-blue one, which Solly returned to Nordstrom's.

On New Year's Day, 2003, Ann goes downtown by subway, then starts walking the few blocks toward the former site of the World Trade Center. The streets are full of tourists all moving in the same direction. It is cold and windy and there is a light snow on the ground. They pass City Hall, many closed office buildings, Trinity Church where a service seems to be going on—Ann hears the thick orotund sounds of organ music. Hot dog vendors are doing a robust business, and she buys a dog with sauerkraut, heavy on the mustard. Despite the

mushy roll, she likes the feel of the warm food in her mouth and belly. Sightseers mill around the jerry-built wooden walls that surround the site. Faded paper flowers festoon the walls, and also worn taped-on photographs of this young girl and that older man and this middle-aged couple, all with their different skin colors and dates of birth, and always the same date of death. She joins a line of people and, as she waits to advance to the lookout area, pulls her scarf up over her cold nose and chin and kneads her gloved fists against each other— she is pleased that she has not gotten mustard on her gloves.

Finally she is at the front of the line and it is her turn to look through the small square opening. At first she makes out nothing but swirling dust and snow far below in the distance. Pressing her forehead against the cold plastic window doesn't help: her breathing fogs it up and she has to clean it off with her glove. Slowly she realizes that she is looking out into a huge hole the sides of which she can't discern. As she squints, she spots a few yellow construction trucks, dwarf sized, down at the bottom of the pit. Nothing else. It is as if she were looking at an abandoned planet where the soil is eroded and a sandstorm is in progress.

She tries to call up dancing with Matt at Windows on the World, looking out at the city from their lamplit table. They spent every anniversary there, for twenty years. But nothing comes to her. She looks down at the hole, which is all she sees. Behind her, someone yells out, "Hey up there, get a move on! It's cold as a witch's teat!" She continues to look down, and still the towers do not reappear.

NIGHT CALL

THE ANSWERING SERVICE phoned him at two o'clock in the morning. A woman named Rose Petrovich or Petrush, the operator hadn't caught the name exactly, had called. It was an emergency, a death.

"A death? Who's this message for? I'm Dan Dorenbusch, the obstetrician. The gynecologist." In the dark, he ran though a mental list of his patients, all stable. Dan fumbled with his penlight, shook it until the batteries made contact and the minuscule light went on. Beside him his sleeping wife mumbled something, turned away, drifted to the far side of the bed. Still half asleep himself, he took down the area code—a New Jersey area code—and phone number, and hung up. Maybe the caller wanted his father, who was a pediatrician in East Orange.

Almost before Dan finished dialing the number, a woman was whispering and sobbing into the telephone, words and wails and a sputtering sound of *s*'s tumbling over each other like roiling water. "He's dead. He's dead. Your father's dead."

"Who is this?" he whispered. "What are you talking about?" He strained to hear as though there were static on the line.

"Your father's dead! Sam's dead! Can you come here? Please! My son's asleep downstairs."

"What? What? Who are you? What is this?"

"It's Rosemarie. Rosemarie Petrowski, your father's receptionist, his nurse. Sam's dead!"

Dan had an urge to cry *April Fools!* and laugh uproariously, except it was July. Cut the crap, he wanted to insist, and put my mother on the phone. Although he knew very well that the number he had called was not his parents', he imagined the nurse setting the telephone down on the familiar hall table and walking through his parents' large dark house to wake his mother. Go on, go get her, he wanted to shout. But he sat in silence watching the fluorescent second hand slowly sweep around the face of the bedside clock. Minesweeper, he thought, absurdly.

Certain "reasonable" questions bobbled in his mind— what's his pulse? his respirations? can you get his blood pressure?—and then disappeared.

Oh Rose-Marie, I love you.
I'm always dreaming of you.

On the other end the nurse was crying.

"Shhh, shhh," he said foolishly. "You mustn't cry. You'll wake my wife." He could see her stirring, starting to turn toward him, and he mumbled "Sorry, sorry," and walked cautiously out of the bedroom, past the children's rooms to the kitchen, where he took directions, the white telephone a strange thing in his strange hand. He half heard, half remembered that his father's nurse had a mild speech defect, a sibilant *s*. Now she sounded like a steam radiator whistling at him about the West Side Highway, the New Jersey Turnpike, this street, that street, some of which he knew, having grown up nearby, but he wrote it all down. Beige clapboard house, Walt Disney statues—statues?—in the backyard.

He phoned the garage for his car, then returned to the dark bedroom, where he dressed as if for work—suit, shirt, tie. His wife murmured a sleepy "Bye, dear," and resumed her gentle, even breathing.

Why hadn't he asked the nurse what his father was doing at her place at this time of night? Why hadn't Dan asked the nurse anything, he who asked patients if they used drugs and how many sexual partners they had, and whether their husbands had relations with men?

The roads were empty. He sped through the hot night but he had the feeling that he was plodding, that the air had thickened into sludge.

Who was this hissing woman whom he'd seen over the years at his father's office without especially noticing her? She had seemed a bit older than Dan, perhaps in her mid-fifties, or maybe she seemed older because her hair had gray in it, and she was mildly overweight, albeit shapely. His mother had complained she said "eck setera" and "for him and I." Sum total of his memories, except Rosemarie had once made him a sandwich and a good cup of coffee at the office and unobtrusively exchanged Dan's father's full ashtray for a clean one.

As he drove, the red numbers of his expensive digital watch—a present from his father—flashed 2:14:40:9, the tenths of seconds rolling over each other, the seconds running, the minutes. He was warm and clammy despite the blasting air conditioner.

As instructed, he pulled into the third driveway on the north side of the block and turned off his lights. Automatically, he pulled out the emergency kit he kept under his seat, trying to remember what he had in there ... CPR face shield, suture stuff, forceps ...

It was a bright night, the sky white with stars. White-hot. He walked quickly past the statues of a faun and Snow White and a number of dwarfs—Jesus! Were all seven of them really there, Happy and Dopey and whoever? White dwarfs ... disintegrating stars. How peculiar that the universe contained billions of stars in billions of constellations, in billions of galaxies. Every star had to die. Although it was a short walk, his shirt felt damp against his chest by the time he entered the house.

She had left the side door open for him and a small light on in the muggy kitchen. There was a portable TV on the kitchen table, and the walls, of pasteboard paneling meant to look like knotty pine, were dotted with picture postcards and articles ripped out of newspapers. The close air smelled of beer and cigars.

He turned left and moved quickly to the living room, where her son—she'd told Dan—was sleeping on the couch. What was his name? Alan? Albert? Dan had seen him once years ago at the office reading a comic book. And to Dan's relief, a long thin boy who looked to be fourteen was, in fact, stretched out there asleep, mouth breathing, a bare foot on the coffee table where a plastic fan clattered. Beside it a sandwich lay half eaten on a paper plate along with a full glass of milk.

Dan carried his kit (the metal box was slippery now—he stopped a second to wipe his hands on his pants) up the narrow noisy staircase to the second floor. In the dark hallway there was a thin strip of light from ceiling to floor where a door was open a crack.

He pushed it open wider and entered the small bedroom. At once he became aware of an unpleasant, sweetish-sharp smell in the air. He looked around quickly, wrinkling up his nose in the heat. At the far end of the small room on a dark dresser sat a plastic tray of perfume bottles and scattered hairpins, and a bra, the cups of which stood up. A man's trousers and knit shirt lay rumpled over the back of the one chair and on the floor nearby were a pair of shimmery green-gold silk boxers. A large fan whirred in the window, blowing the white curtains into the room. Two small lamps, the only sources of light, stood on the night tables on either side of the double bed, which looked freshly made with white sheets and a white eyelet cover pulled tight.

For an instant Dan had the thought that he was alone in this peculiar house except for the boy downstairs, that it was a prank some spiteful patient had pulled and here he was carrying his emergency kit into a strange bedroom in the middle of the night looking for all he knew like a burglar, or a murderer who couldn't make up his mind about his weapon.

Then he saw her sitting on the floor on the other side of the bed almost in the corner, her back up against the wall, her head bowed. Her hair was harsh blue black now, stuck to her round face, her dark eyes were downcast, and under her bright orangey lipstick—it seemed freshly applied, the brightest thing in the place except for the green-gold boxer shorts—her lips looked swollen, her nose was gashed. Over a pajama top, she wore her open nurse-receptionist's white coat, ROSEMARIE embroidered on the pocket in script.

As she made no sign of being aware of Dan's presence, he walked quickly around the foot of the bed. There on the floor, covered to his neck with a bedspread, lay his father, his head cradled in her lap, his forehead leaning up against her belly protruding in tight jeans; she was caressing his cheeks and his chin. For an instant Dan looked away, attended to the pale-blue shiny acetate fabric of the bedspread, as if it were the center of the scene.

Then he knelt and felt for his father's pulse at his cool throat and at his wrist, which seemed warm. Had she been holding it? His father's pupils were large and black, looking at nothing. From his jacket pocket Dan pulled out his penlight and shone it in his father's eyes. Two stones. Although it made no sense, he yanked off the bedspread and, looking away from his father's lax glistening penis curved on the dark scrotum, hauled him away from Rosemarie by the ankles. She grunted in surprise. Had she not kept her hands under his father's head, Dan would have banged it on the floor. He pulled his father's undershirt up—the thing was on inside out with the label under his father's chin—and, with his hands joined in a fist, smashed down as hard as he could at the midpoint of his father's chest. He banged down twice more and thought he heard or felt a rib crack. He pressed his ear very tightly against the cool chest wall. He could hear his own blood racing in his ear as if he were listening to a seashell. He banged again and again and again and stopped only when Rosemarie threw her arms around his father's chest. Dan pushed her away roughly and listened. The empty shell.

He drew the bedspread back up. Dan shut his father's eyes and closed his own and sat outside the arc of light thrown by the small bedside lamp and after a while heard himself say the first line of the Shema, all he knew: "*Shema Yisrael Adonai Eloheinu Adonai Echad.*" Hear O Israel the Lord our God the Lord is One. He was surprised to hear himself say it because he didn't believe in God.

After a moment Dan opened his eyes and looked at the slack skin of his father's neck, at his prominent cheekbones. Tatar cheekbones. One of his father's eyes was narrower than the other, as if he had been punched, and the tissues had begun to swell. Dan looked at Rosemarie's "peasant face," his mother had once called it, to his father's annoyance. "Pleasant face," his father had corrected her. It was a pleasant face still, despite the sag at the chin: all the features were full, soft, rounded, even the lines at the corners of her eyes and mouth curved upwards. Dan saw now that her lower lip was indeed swollen, bruised, the skin of her nose torn.

He looked back at his father's narrowed eye. There was a cluster of broken blood vessels under it, on his father's right cheek.

Dan sat down on the bed, his eyes intent on her face. "What happened? What happened here?"

She inched down a little to where his father lay and took his head in her lap again.

"I need to know." He knew. He didn't know. "Don't be a prude. Were you into S&M? I'm a gynecologist—believe me, I've seen everything."

She glared at Dan. "He had a fit! A huge seizure! I'm lucky I didn't get my skull fractured!"

"How could he have a seizure? He wasn't an epileptic."

"You tell me. You're the doctor."

"Just give me the sequence of events." He tried to gentle his voice. "Anything. This is terrible"—then he forced himself to add—"for both of us."

She looked at his father's head in her lap and began to cry.

He waited for what seemed a long time, although his watch indicated only two minutes had passed. "Anything. Tell me anything at all." His voice surprised him—there was a tone of real sympathy in it.

Finally, when she began to speak, she did not look at him, seemed to be talking to his father, whose head rested in her lap. "We were, we were—" She touched her fingertips together and bounced them against each other several times and then clasped her hands shut. "He came by around twelve. We drank some beer. Ali's asleep downstairs, so we never sit there long— usually just till your father unwinds. We watched maybe fifteen minutes of TV. An old movie." She paused for a moment and twirled an index and third finger back and forth around each other as if they were dancing. "*Gigi*," she finally got out, "with Leslie Caron."

Usually. Never. The words sounded strange to him, foreign. Although she spoke softly, they boomed ominously, battering rams.

"We—came—up here. He was edgy because he missed a diagnosis of AIDS in an infant. Someone else caught it, but Sam felt humiliated. I tell you, he looked fine! Not sick at all! I talked about the trouble my boy's been having at school. He said he'd get Ali some tutoring—" She began to cry again, her shoulders hunched in the white coat. She rocked back and forth. After a while, still leaning over his dead father, she dried her eyes with the bedspread.

"We—we—we got out of—" She waved an arm at the dresser and chair where their clothes lay. "He was waiting— waiting for me . . . " She smiled at the dead man tenderly.

As what she was saying began to sink in, Dan's hot face heated up further.

"He started telling me this joke about the Germans starting a sex school during the Second World War. For making babies. And they had a graduating class and they were asking the girls who they wanted to father their kids . . . Suddenly your father opened his mouth wide—and made high yipping noises and choking sounds, and his eyes were tearing"—she shut her eyes tight—"and I thought, like an idiot, he's really into this joke. 'Shhhush, shhhush,' I say. 'Ali's sleeping.'" She looked apprehensively at the door now as if she expected to see her son there any minute. Then she looked at Dan. "He had a big seizure. He started thrashing around on top of me. I thought he'd break my nose." Then she began to cry again and buried her face in his father's chest. Dan felt an urge to lift her up—whether to comfort her or to get her off his father he wasn't sure.

She sat up, her hands still on his father's chest, her fingers rolling and unrolling his gray chest hairs as she spoke. "He had an airway so I pounded on his chest and breathed for him. I went on for a good twenty minutes. Afterwards I sponged him down." She inclined her head toward a metal bowl of washcloths and soapy water on the floor under the window. Beside it was a box of Ivory Flakes and he thought that maybe she was proud, wanted him to know that she had changed the sheets before Dan arrived and aired everything out. Next to the box of soap stood a can that looked like air spray, which probably accounted for the sweet chemical odor in the room—and she had combed his father's thin hair and at least gotten the undershirt on.

Dan watched her crying quietly. She was sitting just as she had been when Dan entered the room, her back against the wall, her head inclined toward his father's head in her lap, her fingers feeling their way over his dark face. And Dan realized he felt completely strange before this woman, who was grieving for his father whom she had loved, it seemed, and who had perhaps loved her, for years.

He thought again of touching her shoulder. He thought of telling her the rest of that joke—the star pupil wanted Churchill to be the father of her child because she'd heard him say, "Eet veell be long and it veell be hard. Ve veell do it on the rooftops, ve veell do it on the beachheads . . ." He thought of helping her off with her receptionist's coat and her tight pair of jeans and getting into her where his father had just been warm and alive. (Had he come, the poor bastard? No, he'd apparently missed out, but only that last once.) Should he slap this woman around out of respect for his mother? He'd never slapped anyone around, let alone a woman.

His eyes dry and gritty, Dan sat motionless on the bed.

They dressed his father, Rosemarie getting the undershirt off and back on right side out, label in back, while Dan hoisted up the dead man's heavy chest at the armpits. He was repelled at touching his father's buttocks, at grazing his sparse gray pubic hair with his hand as he helped her shimmy up the green-gold boxers. They spent a quarter of an hour lifting and rolling his father's dead weight into his cotton slacks and the maroon knit shirt with the alligator on the pocket. Rosemarie couldn't find his socks. She said she had extras, but Dan shook his head, feeling some distaste about actually seeing the drawer (drawers?) where his father kept his things. (Just how much clothing did his father have here? Besides being in each other's company all day at the office, had they gone out evenings, gone dancing? What did they do, whatever did they do?) He looked under the bed with his penlight for the socks (only dust there), looked in the disordered bathroom (open lipstick containers and soiled cotton puffs on the counter), and in the stuffed hamper. Finally, although it seemed a mistake, he just put his father's sandals on his bare feet.

Then they moved slowly, jerkily, down the stairs, Rosemarie walking backwards holding the feet, Dan holding the torso at the armpits, feeling the weight in his lower back, at the same place he felt it when he bent over to do a pelvic or pull out a kid. He had the strange thought that he was really helping carry a chest of drawers, or a couch, and he should have hired movers. Had Dan renewed his disability coverage? This could lay him up for weeks.

Did his father have any life insurance, had he left anything for his mother? Pediatricians were the worst-paid doctors, right down there with psychiatrists. And his father was an improvident type, had been involved in one bad business scheme after another—once Dan's mother's piano had been carted off, supposedly to pay debts, and another time his father almost lost the house. Circumstances of death the only thing he had in common with Rockefeller.

In the dark, one of his father's arms made a dull wooden sound as it collided with the banister. Dan signaled to Rosemarie. While he rested against the banister for a moment listening to her son's even breathing below, listening to their own harsher breathing and at the same time trying to figure out how in God's name he might earn a few extra thousand bucks a month for his mother (Dan almost groaned aloud), he watched Rosemarie set his father's legs down carefully on the steps, then try to fold the arms up on the chest. But they were unyielding, two poles.

Still no sound from his father.

Suddenly on the dark stairway Dan was gasping for air. He wanted to shout out that he was alive, he was suffocating, he would collapse and fall down the stairs . . .

Rosemarie whispered, "Are you all right?"

He held up one finger to indicate he needed a minute, then sat down on the stairs, holding his father's head in his lap. Dan forced himself to take slow shallow breaths, build up some carbon dioxide in his bloodstream. He was breathing like a tornado, hyperventilating. He mustn't faint, mustn't leave her alone.

After a few moments he felt less woozy, although mildly ashamed of himself. Slowly they got the body down the stairs, through the kitchen, where Dan noticed again the picture postcards tacked haphazardly to the fake wood paneling. He suddenly wondered if they could be from places his father and Rosemarie had visited together—his father had attended a lot of professional meetings. Dan remembered receiving a post-card of a silver beach in Acapulco—was that where some pediatric association had held its meeting? Had he considered going (there were some neonatal talks, if he had the right meeting) but his father dissuaded him?

They carried the body out the back door, down the steps, and pushing and pulling and yanking, hiked it onto the front seat of Dan's car. Dan sat rigid behind the wheel. If he was rigid, he couldn't faint, right? Rosemarie was in the passenger seat by the window, his father in a sort of slumped-back position between them, legs hardly bent. Dan kept an arm like a strap across the dead man's chest. Rosemarie got his father's head close to her shoulder, as if he were asleep or drunk. She held his father's hand.

Although Dan wanted to floor the accelerator, he drove slowly through the deserted side streets. Rosemarie and he did not speak. They passed a police car parked beside the golf course, a policeman in the front seat with a bleached blonde whose hair seemed to be burning in the dark. They were smoking and they paid no attention to Dan.

I am in bed asleep beside my sleeping wife.

His wife would think he'd gone berserk and maybe he had, because otherwise what was he doing out here in the middle of the mad night slithering past the orthodontist's office where he'd had his braces applied as a boy ("Are those tears coming out your eyes? They'll be coming out your ears before I'm done with you," Dr. Heller, the orthodontist, had said as he tightened the fifteen-year-old's braces, and Dan had never told his father from fear he'd kill Dr. Heller); past the squat candy—now video—store behind which Dan and two buddies had smoked their first cigarettes ("They're for my father," Dan, who'd been delegated to buy the pack, had offered unasked, pronouncing them "Pell Mells," as in the old

television commercial); past the turreted junior high school
with its black playing fields and tennis courts where Dan had
won (unseen by his father, who had been suturing a boy's torn
lip, or so he'd said) the Under-Fifteen Rough Riders Tennis
Tournament.

Had his father been carrying on with Rosemarie way back
then? No, impossible, Rosemarie had been only a girl herself.
But had there been others? For God's sake, was that boy, that
Ali, his half brother? No, no. Rosemarie had been married to
a male nurse and had a child, this child, and later got a divorce.
Dan was almost sure. Besides, she'd said "*my* boy."

Well, what was she supposed to say?

Had his mother kept her eyes deliberately shut? She'd
fought a deep-freeze war with his father all her life, and this
escalation, if known to her, would have atomized the marriage.
Besides, his mother would never have stood for his father's
having any pleasure.

Dousing his headlights, Dan pulled onto the noisy gravel
driveway, then watched Rosemarie's largish—voluptuous?—
can sway in the white coat as she made her way to the rear
door of the flagstone house that had served as his father's
office. Zaftig, his father had called her without Dan's picking
up on anything: his father was always commenting on women's
bodies—TV actresses, waitresses, store clerks, passersby.

Dan's wife's body.

As he watched Rosemarie lean over the lock, he wondered
what there had been between her and his father besides the
old in-and-out: Camaraderie? Passion? Love? What went on
between a man and a woman who was twenty years younger?
If his father had wanted Dan to know, he would have told

him himself. Or maybe he *had* tried to tell Dan, and Dan had
failed to decipher the code. As he watched Rosemarie now
returning to the car, her layers of clothes sticking to her so that
every curvy curve was thrown into bold white relief, Dan
remembered his father once mentioning that his nurse sweated
like a basketball player.

Dan got out of the car, and he and Rosemarie carried the
body across the driveway, barely managing to keep it above the
gravel. How could it be so hot so early in the morning? How
unreal, how numb he felt! His thoughts seemed to be occur-
ring at a certain physical distance from his head, as if they
weren't his or were stillborn at the moment he thought them.
Suddenly he felt terrified he would drop to his knees holding
his father and howl. Without giving any warning, he began to
walk faster, almost to run, and Rosemarie tripped and nearly
fell. "Sorry, sorry," he whispered.

Inside they hoisted the body onto a child-size gurney,
which they wheeled through the dark storage room, Dan
training the beam of his small light in front of Rosemarie,
who moved cartons of supplies and stacks of records out of
their way. One of his father's feet pointed uncomfortably
close to Dan's crotch. They proceeded past the examining
rooms, into his father's office, where the facade of the Basilica
of San Marco glittered from the surface of his desk. (His
father'd bought that garish desk in Venice maybe five years
ago. Hadn't there been a symposium in Venice, hadn't Dan
gotten a postcard?) Dan eased his father into his leather chair,
Rosemarie guiding the head carefully down onto the shining
desktop.

Her own head slumped over as if she were mirroring

the dead man. "Do you think if we hadn't been—do you think if we'd stayed watching television?—this wouldn't have happened?"

Although he had wondered himself, he smiled uncomfortably. "People can get pretty excited watching television." To stop smiling (although she probably couldn't see his face), he frowned. "He must have thrown an embolus into his brain, or he ruptured a major vessel."

"You think so?" Her head rose a bit.

"Well, I've seen a sudden death from an embolus—an amniotic fluid embolus, but it should work the same way." By its whiteness Dan found a lab coat in his father's closet and took it off the hanger. Aiming his small light at his father and laying it on the desk, he began pushing one of his father's cool hands into the sleeve of the lab coat. While he whispered professorially at her (he *was* whispering, wasn't he, not howling?) about the circulation of blood in the brain, Dan fed the shoulder in, threaded his father's stiffened hand down and out the sleeve.

Rosemarie said, "Do you think if I'd injected epinephrine directly into the heart? I mean, if I'd had it in the house."

"You wouldn't have done him any favor. He must have suffered massive brain damage."

"You think so?" Rosemarie asked almost eagerly, turning fully toward Dan, who was working the other shoulder into the coat. "What are you doing?" She sounded as if she had just now noticed.

"We want the police to think he came in because he was worried about some patient, maybe that baby with AIDS. He looked at some slides. He sat down at his desk. He dropped dead. Where does he keep the slides? Still in the kitchen?"

"What do you need the lab coat for?"

Dan shrugged his shoulders. "You look at slides, you wear a lab coat."

"Sam was hardly a stickler for details."

"What do you need yours for?"

She looked at her white coat and the pajama top beneath it. He imagined her flushing.

"It'll authenticate the story," he said, although he was not sure what story he was authenticating. As he got the other arm through, he blurted out, "Does my mother know?"

"I don't think so. I don't think they talk enough for her to know anything." Rosemarie sounded bitter, as if she were personally affronted by the relationship between his parents.

"It was kind of you to call me." He looked away.

"I was thinking about Ali, about his waking up with Sam dead there, the police. He was very fond of your father." Her voice wavered. "Do you know they played baseball together? Your dad took him to a few Yankees games."

He never took *me* to any Yankees games.

Embarrassed, as if she could read his mind, he quickly said, "Look, we need some kind of story for the police. In case my mother doesn't know. I could say he was in the office working late and he called me because he felt acutely ill and I drove out and found him."

In the dark Dan raised his own objections: "They'll ask why didn't I call 911, or the ambulance or whoever you call out here . . . Why didn't *you* call 911?"

"*I am* 911," she said. "I go out with the ambulance."

A low farting noise sounded from the body. Dan picked up his father's wrist and felt for a pulse. The sound erupted

again—a gurgle—and a dark stain began to spread from the
seat of his father's pants, down one leg, and onto the industrial
gray carpet. He wanted to throw a cover, some kind of shield
over his father. In the dark his father's forehead seemed ash
colored, his elbow was gashed, and the back of his maroon
shirt was torn and dirty beneath the lab coat. Although he
knew the provenance of every bruise—that he himself must
have gashed his father's elbow when he dragged him across the
driveway, Dan found himself wondering why he had accepted
this woman's story so readily. Someone walking in might think
the two of them had rolled and killed the old man. Rolled
him for his debts. Probably left a mountain of them. "He looks
like a murdered derelict."

Rosemarie began to wail.

He rose on tiptoe, moved his finger stupidly to his lips lest
he wail himself. He tried not to imagine the tears coursing
down her face, dampening her starched coat.

"There must be another shirt around." He began riffling
through his father's desk drawers pointing the flashlight.

"Leave him alone, it's enough." Still crying, she started for
the door.

"We have to have a story for the police." He felt like a
determined lunatic. Having found a wrinkled short-sleeved
cotton shirt in a drawer, he began trying to get his father's lab
coat off. Papers fell off the desk and onto the floor.

"I'm going home. Maybe my boy is awake."

Dan grabbed her wrist. With his other hand he stood
holding the short-sleeved shirt.

She said simply, "I'll tell the police not to say anything to
your mother, if that's what your worry is."

"Don't they have to write the circumstances and the place on the death certificate?"

"Not the circumstances. The place, yes, and the time. They'll approximate the time. Look, everyone knows me," she said. "The police, the undertaker—Buddy Lerner's the undertaker. I've known him since fourth grade. I'll ask him to do me a favor."

Just like that? Dan had to figure this out. "It'll take only a few minutes to get off his lab coat and change his shirt and wash his face."

"Who you kidding? Let go of me, I want to go home."

Surprised that he was still holding on to her wrist, and also, it seemed, to her waist, to her warm flesh, of course he released her.

"I can clean him up in the morning," she continued. "I'll find him in the morning when I come in to work and I'll tell everyone he must have had a stroke."

"And a seizure. And you tried to resuscitate him. Banged him up more."

"Okay. The truth. A seizure and a stroke."

"But you have to have his car here. You can't have his body here and his car at your place."

She nodded. "I'll drive it over in the morning. Let go of me."

"I'm not touching you." He moved several steps away to make sure she saw he had let her go. "But what about *your* car? How will they think you got to work?"

She felt through his father's pants pockets and slapped the keys into Dan's hand.

He drove her home. When she got out of the car and walked up the dark steps to her house, he felt unspeakably lonely.

He found his father's leased red Jaguar parked two blocks from her house. The car was a beacon, a torch, he would be stopped by the police—he felt a spurt of fear that momentarily overcame his loneliness as he drove the car to the office and left it in the driveway.

It was an hour's walk back to Rosemarie's. He walked briskly along the finally cooling suburban streets, the white flowering magnolia trees lit up ghostly in the graying dark, past the golf course, the green smell of black grass. He had a sudden memory of prairies, of a childhood vacation out west. It was one of the few vacations his busy father had been able to take—he was always at the hospital, making house calls, talking on the phone to other doctors . . . Dan had spent his childhood yearning for his father. His mother had stayed in the hotel the afternoon he and his father had visited the thousands-of-feet-high ruined dwellings of the Anasazi Indians. Standing holding his father's big hand at the edge of the cliff with the bright blue cloudless sky and orange sun above them, he'd had the commonplace thought that if they made one misstep, his beloved father and he would fall to their deaths together. It had been an awful but thrilling thought.

And now his father had died alone. No, not alone. Without him. With another.

He heard the sounds of hundreds of frogs from the golf course. He heard his footsteps. Although he was exhausted, he knew he could not sleep. He wondered was anyone lying awake in the houses he passed, was anyone listening to his footsteps, watching him through a window? He wondered how it could be that his eyes were as dry as if the tear ducts had been cut out of them, and he was walking along a street at five thirty in the morning wondering if anyone was hearing him, if anyone was watching him. Was his father watching him?

Back at his own car, for an instant he imagined himself running up the stairs and embracing Rosemarie, holding tight to her forever.

But he saw the bicycle on her front lawn and how dark, how dark her house was, and he turned away.

ARTIFACT

For Jo

S HE DID NOT want to disturb the rats. Breathing "Lullaby,
and good night," trying to keep the wire cage in her arms
steady, she walked down the dimly lit hall. The lab equipment
was turned off for the weekend and there was no sound except
for the soft, slapping noise of her slippers and her low song.
Occasionally a rat lifted his head and sniffed the air.

Lottie worked in a pair of cutoff jeans and a T-shirt her
gross anatomy class had given her, which showed the muscles
of the chest and back labeled in Latin. Her hair was piled up
on top of her head with a lab clamp.

The radio said it was the hottest August night since 1983.
On the highways to Long Island and the Jersey Shore the
traffic had been bumper to bumper all day, the cars bulging
with sun umbrellas, baby carriages, bicycles tied to roofs. After
dinner when she took a break to walk toward Central Park in
search of a breeze, the close streets seemed to her vacant and
forlorn. The charged life of the city dimmed in August. Most
of her colleagues were on vacation; during the day a few technicians came in, the department secretary, occasionally a
worried graduate student.

She liked being alone in her lab in the hushed city, undisturbed by the rhythms of others, a pleasure she didn't experience often now that she had small children again. Simon was two and Davy was six, and they were wild bucking things. Her eighteen-year-old, Lila, usually had friends over; they sat in Lottie's study working on her computer or making clothes for college on her sewing machine. Her husband, Jake, had private music students weekday afternoons and on Saturdays. And in August his fourteen-year-old daughter, Ruth, blew in from LA like a small high-pressure front. She danced and cooked for her dad, ignoring the boys and taking jabs and pokes at her stepmother. Lottie tried to schedule a major experiment every August.

On the counter the caged rats shifted restlessly in the moonlight.

She switched on the tensor lamp at the dissecting table and the light above the sink, tied herself into an old surgical gown, drew on a workman's glove, and ran the cold water. She slipped open the lid of a cage, gripped the nearest quivering animal, and lifted it out. She raised the paper-cutter blade and positioned the animal's head on the platform, his squirming body just off the edge. His pink feet kicked the air. He began defecating black pellets, urinating in spasms on her glove. She brought the blade down, crunching through the bottom of his neck. The head lay on the platform. Lottie held tight to the body, which continued to struggle, spraying blood through the open neck. Her cheek was suddenly wet. Thrusting the body under the cold water, she held on until it quieted and stopped. Then she dumped it into a plastic bag and laid the head on the dissecting table. She shook the glove off and, taking up the scalpel and forceps, dissected out the sublingual and submandibular salivary glands, easing them into a beaker of fixative. She washed her face and reached into the cage for the next rat.

She liked to set a rhythm, do what had to be done steadily and speedily. The smell of blood was in the room now and the rats knew. They squawked even before she reached for them and no matter how firmly she held on, they wouldn't lie still. In the air-conditioned room she was sweating.

Lottie had been intermittently irritable the last few months, ever since a microscopy journal that had solicited a paper from her had sent it back for extensive revisions. She had developed new techniques for spotlighting each organelle of a particular cell in the salivary gland, the function of which no one understood, although it was implicated in several diseases, one of them fatal.

The journal's referees had savaged her paper, from the typing to the heart of the work: she was not describing the actual cell at all, nor the real components of the mucus, but only the distortions created by the very techniques she was advocating. One critic finished up:

> This paper is not acceptable for publication since it is replete with accidental and random findings. It is no more than a collection of artifacts.

She read the lines twice, then crushed the reports into a ball and stuffed it into the bottom drawer of her desk.

A month later a small grant proposal of hers was rejected.

A colleague said, if only she'd cited a few of the committee members' papers, or had had key people and their wives over for drinks . . .

The following week her chair phoned her. He had heard about the grant and thought it was unjust. She was one of the most productive people in the department, with a bibliography second in length and quality only to his own. The graduate students stood on line for her seminar. She was innovative, she was creative. Unfortunately, he had bad news for her himself.

"No raise," Lottie said.

He was terribly sorry. She must be aware she was on a frozen budget line. Actually they were all small animals caught in a glacier, if he could speak for a moment from the paleontological point of view. The city was cutting back, the NIH was tightening its belt, there was nothing he could do. Next year it would be a different ball game; she could rest assured he'd go to bat for her then.

It was the third year he'd handed her that wilted bunch of metaphors and her husband told her to sue. "It's discrimination against women and you're just sitting back and taking it." He cited a well-known microbiologist, a woman, who'd said in a recent *New York Times* article, "Women scientists have two choices: bitterness or foolishness."

Lottie said she wasn't famous enough to make resounding judgments, and if she let herself get involved with lawyers, she wouldn't get her work done.

Jake said, "At least go to the grievance committee. There must be a grievance committee. We need the money."

"I'm not licking ass."

"Who asked you to lick ass? Go in and *yell.* You're not *yelling,* you only yell at me."

Her paper was never far from her mind. The editor had heard her deliver it at the cell biology meetings in Cincinnati six months earlier. The referees were independent of him; still there shouldn't be such a disparity in their opinions. Could her oral presentation have been so much better than her written one?

Her papers were almost always published, but they were invariably sent back for rewriting. Meticulous in conceptualizing problems and running experiments, she was impatient when it came to presenting results, as if to linger over the final draft made her a cosmetician or an interior decorator, not a scientist. In her diagrams she rarely labeled everything that needed labeling; she expected her typists to correct her misspellings and not add any of their own; and she wrote up her conclusions in a matter-of-fact way. Many of her colleagues took some obvious point and polished it up, surrounded it with five or six true but tried ideas that were in the public domain, then passed off this rearrangement as dazzling new stuff. She came with the real thing in a crumpled brown wrapper. And she did it obstinately, insisting to herself that there was virtue in such a presentation.

One evening in June she took the paper ball out of the drawer she'd buried it in. As she unfolded and smoothed out the sheets on her desk, the sound in the still lab was like a crackling fire.

There are quite a number of typing errors, etc., which I
have marked in pencil . . . A significant problem with this
paper is that the description of the author's methodologies
is far too skimpy. We are not told the source of the glutaral-
dehyde; the osmolality of the individual fixatives; the length
of time these were applied.

Skimming over the pages, she saw that many of the objections
were of this order, but one referee had a major substantive
disagreement. Her point had been that different fixatives and
buffers preserved different aspects of the cell, just as various
experiences brought out various aspects of a human being: with
a cell, one could choose a fixative and buffer according to which
aspects one hoped to illuminate. The referee wanted her to use
other fixatives and buffers, claiming that hers damaged the cell
contents while the ones he suggested would preserve them
"correctly." She knew they would just do different damage. It was
as if he believed that there was a proper way of looking at a cell.

Another referee objected to her manner of sacrificing rats.
She had killed them first and then dissected out the salivary
glands and placed them in fixative. This referee thought that in
the few minutes between death and the fixative, the glands
underwent permanent distorting changes and hence what she
had reported was "mere artifact." He wanted her to inject the
fixative into the living animals. Early on, before deciding on
her current method, she had in fact killed a few rats by fixing
them alive. The results were no more "natural" and the technique took more time and was more unpleasant.

To get the paper published, at least in this journal, she would
have to run the whole experiment again, probably several

times, killing rats in a variety of ways, using a number of unnecessary fixatives. It would be tedious. She was working on
another project. Rats didn't grow on trees, nor did technician
time. Her chest tightened as she thought of going to the
university treasurer, that cheery bureaucrat, justifying the cost
of each rat to him, putting her crumpled referees' reports in
his hands. She felt like punching someone.

In the end she phoned her chair and cajoled and shamed him
into giving her the money out of the department slush fund.

Then she typed each of the referees' objections on a separate
sheet of paper and taped them up on her lab walls. As the
results came in, she posted them in black on the sheets if the
referees were right, in red magic marker if she was right. Her
handwriting was large and flowery, full of swirls and curlicues,
and she often had to add several pages to the original one in
order to fit everything in. By the end of July, the walls were
festooned with poinsettias and bright clusters of holly berries;
the place looked like Christmas. She had two colleagues check
her work, although she intended to run the experiment once
more in August. Lottie cheered up.

She found herself imagining bits of letters to the editor
who had twice urged her to revise and resubmit. She had her
hand in the hot tub water, testing it for her sons:

I regret not answering earlier but I have been immersed
in an important experiment.

The boys, covered with washable finger paints and standing
by with gunboats and water pistols, jumped in and sent the
water level over the top.

I have not answered sooner because I have been flooded with requests for this particular paper and am considering sending it to the *International Journal of Cell Research* instead.

As she bathed her boisterous blue-and-yellow sons, she refuted each objection the anonymous referees had made. She scrubbed and rubbed and rinsed them back to flesh color. She toweled them dry and handed them over to her husband, then sat down at the computer and shot off a letter to that editor:

> Beyond all the verification and justification of my techniques are two issues which are fundamental. The first is the whole point of the paper, which the reviewers seem to have missed: namely, that there is no "correct" morphology of the granules in this gland, but rather that the fixative, buffer, and additive combination will determine which constituents will be preserved, which destroyed. The other issue is philosophical and has to do with the concept of artifact. It should be clear to anyone with experience in this business that all one ever deals with is artifact, and that one's skills in creating and interpreting artifact are largely the measure of one's abilities as a morphologist/scientist. From my perspective the issue is not, is a given structure artifact? But rather, can the conditions under which a given artifact is produced provide information about the actual nature of a particular organism which cannot be analyzed in its natural form? We are dealing with a biological equivalent of the uncertainty principle, and all fine-structural morphologists and cytochemists should be aware of that.

Jake brought her a cold glass of seltzer with a piece of lime. "Everyone asleep?" she said.

"You kidding?" He kissed his wife's damp forehead. "Tell me when you're done," he said. "All the stars are out."

The night watchman had come and gone. Lottie took off her gown and put it in a shopping bag along with a dirty lab coat and a pair of thick socks she'd had around since the winter; she would run them through the washing machine at home. She usually did the lab wash late at night or early in the morning when the kids were asleep; she didn't like them getting a look or a whiff. Although she'd sponged down the countertops twice, the room still smelled of blood and urine and fixative. She washed the counters again. Not cautious by nature, in the lab she was painstaking and unforgiving with those who were not. A graduate student had once left a highly corrosive solution in an open beaker and the janitor had knocked it over and then mopped it up with paper towels; he needed skin grafting on his fingers. The day after she visited the janitor in the hospital, Lottie told the student she wouldn't work with him anymore, and he had to get a new thesis topic and adviser.

She carried the plastic garbage bag of rat parts into the cold room. Except for a few cats and a rare monkey, most of the black bags here contained rat corpses—rats who'd had tumors implanted in their heads, who'd breathed in cigarette smoke every hour of their short lives, who'd eaten their weight in saccharin and sodium nitrates, who'd had their fetuses androgenized and estrogenized *in utero*. She thought what unimaginable, un-rat-like destinies these animals had had—we should build a monument to them in every city.

Strands of hair escaped from her makeshift upsweep. She tried to blow them away, not wanting to touch her hands to her face. She locked her lab and went to the on-call room, where she showered.

The clean hot water pounding away at her, she looked at her body with some curiosity and no great sense of familiarity, as if she were a cadaver for the medical students. They'd be lucky to get a forty-year-old woman only a few pounds over-weight—five pounds? ten? (fat was the enemy of the anato-mist, making the field slippery, infiltrating the organs)—with all the main structures in place, nothing worse than a few burns and discolorations on her hands, some gleaming stretch marks on her (still fairly taut) breasts and belly, one long white caesarean scar from her last-born, Simon, who had gone into fetal distress and had had to be scooped out in a hurry. She still worried about him. He was a lively child, always poking around, trying to be as grown-up as his four-years-older brother, and often ending up in trouble. He probably started some intrauterine exploration and got tangled in his umbilical cord. She worried less about Davy. Very smart, he wasn't as malleable, as open, as Simon. But perhaps Davy was the more sensitive of the two and it was because his feelings were so easily hurt that he'd become a little impatient and dogmatic. At six he didn't like ambiguity, he hated not catching on at once, and he clearly preferred teaching to learning. He had lately become very much attached to Jake, imitating the way he walked and talked, and showing a special interest in music.

Lottie wondered sometimes what would happen to these children of hers—not Lila, who was nearly grown up, but these little ones. Lottie was forty and Jake was forty-one.

When you had children in your twenties, it could cross your mind you might not stay together, but you took for granted that you'd both be on earth for all time. Jake's father had died of cancer at forty-one.

Outside the night was hot and airless, as if someone had sucked the atmosphere out of the city with a pump. She carried her laundry bag past the sleeping attendant, a black man in his fifties whose wife had died of leukemia a few months earlier. He sat slack in a folding chair on the sidewalk, all bones and dark hollows, like a reamed-out, abandoned mine. As she tried to ease the old station wagon out of the lot without disturbing him, it backfired sharply—an ominous sound in the city night. The man sprang to embarrassed attention and called out "Night, doc," after her disappearing car. And she cursed Jake, who'd promised to get it fixed, then cursed their finances.

She drove up Amsterdam Avenue, past the dark buildings of Columbia University. It was two thirty in the morning and the stores were dark and gated. Turning with relief onto the West Side Highway, she increased her speed, the dense city receding and thinning out, the Hudson River interposing itself between her and the Palisades, giving her a sudden sense of space and view. In the approaching distance the bridge was two blue-studded mountain peaks that sloped to form a valley between them. Wet warm air was forced in the open windows as she continued to accelerate, an automobile-made breeze: her air conditioner had died a month ago. Few cars passed. In the steamy night, alone on the empty highway, she drove a car cluttered with baby bottles, M&M wrappers, animal crackers, a tube of Lila's candy-pink lipstick, crumpled sheets of music.

Besides her own sizable family, she was accountable for two technicians and three doctoral candidates who were writing theses under her. One of them she had inherited a few months ago from a colleague who'd died. The young man was an abysmal student from Haiti, that tormented country. He had been eight years in the department without bringing his thesis and defense of it to a satisfactory conclusion. Lottie had had dinner at his dingy flat in East Harlem. All evening his wife and six children had tried desperately to please her. Lottie attempted to engage one young boy in a game of pickup sticks but his hands trembled so that they had to quit.

Less troubling but equally binding were her obligations to teach the medical students, to sit on various committees, and to publish.

When all of this had come upon her she didn't know— slowly, imperceptibly, over time, she supposed, like a pound or two gained every year but overlooked, until suddenly one day, for no apparent reason, she came face to face with herself in an inner mirror and saw with surprise a very substantial figure, responsible, solid, a matron. Who, me, Lottie?

Sometimes she thought she'd ended up where she was because of a series of random events, that her career, her life's work, had come about by accident. In an undergraduate endocrine class she had agreed to write a paper on cystic fibrosis, confusing it with fibrocystic disease, which interested her because her mother had it—a common condition that thickened breast tissue into lumps that occasionally felt like cancer. During Lottie's childhood her mother had had three (fortunately benign) biopsies to make the distinction.

Cystic fibrosis damaged the lungs and pancreas of children.

Her professor had sent her to watch the autopsy, her first, of an undersized boy who'd died of it, and she never forgot that light-haired seven-year-old lying like a white water lily in a metal pond, the water swirling around him, ready. She remembered the pathologists leaning over his fragile body with its small distended abdomen, the sad bunch of pediatricians, residents, medical students.

She had learned the electron microscope by another peculiar route. The cell biology professor, an internationally known expert on the new technique, already had a full complement of graduate students and refused to take her on. Then a coup occurred in a small central African country she had never heard of, and one of the professor's graduate students, an African on a government grant, packed up and left despite the university's attempts to dissuade him. She still remembered the photo of him in the campus newspaper, smiling and waving, a black bulky figure bundled up against the Wisconsin winter. She'd gone uneasily to see the professor again, but he said he was holding the African's place until his return. When a week later the man was hanged, she went again. Although it was the middle of the semester, the professor irritably accepted her on condition she finish the African's project: he was working on rat salivary glands.

Although she'd read all the Nancy Drew mysteries as a girl, and exchanged friendship rings and worn fluorescent socks and an Elvis Presley button, and prayed to God that Charlie Hart, who lived around the corner, would fall in love with her, she was also right from the beginning an observant, passionately curious child who lay for hours in summer fields watching the doings of lizards and bugs and worms. Staring through binoculars for a glimpse of a sparrow's eggs hatching, she stayed all day in a tree one time when she was twelve, straining her eyes.

Someone once asked her what had so caught her attention. She was startled by the question. Who would not be interested in seeing sparrows hatch? As an adult, she had come to recognize that most of the world would not be interested. At cocktail parties people were impressed that she was a scientist, but no one wanted to hear exactly what she did. Their eyes glazed over whenever she began to explain, no matter how simply she put things.

Lottie drove off the highway onto a two-lane, nearly unlit road that she knew by heart. It was bordered by large shade trees that arched to form a leafy roof in places; Davy, her six-year-old, called it a "tree tunnel." The air coming in the windows had turned cooler, sweeter; she opened her mouth and breathed it in with her whole body. Although the fields were dark and the huge trees were black shapes faintly outlined in the moonlight, and all she could see was an occasional night-light on the porch of a farmhouse in the distance or lighting up the front room of a gas station, she knew where things were; she could almost take her sights through her pores. It was a soft, familiar darkness.

Where she lived now at forty was a town very much like the one she'd grown up in—rural, supported by farming, Presbyterian, bright with harsh fresh white paint and yellow forsythia and gaudy tiger lilies, plants that made it through hard winters and burst out, when it was time, in pride and self-reliance—even in a kind of fierceness. In the spring the air was suffused with the odor of apple blossoms, a scent that always saddened her, and with the sweet smell of lilacs. Nowadays she was the lady scientist, the one who had kids from two different marriages, and another kid, a dark one, who showed up for half the summer, and a Jew for a husband (though he played Sundays at the church for free), and two ratty cars and a place that needed a paint job and a mow job bad.

As she pulled into their gravel driveway the dogs yapped briefly and then quieted, recognizing whatever modern-day dogs recognize: the rhythm of the mistress's motor? The scent of her buffers and fixatives? She got out of the car and stretched for a moment in the moonlight. The night was dense with tiny intermeshing sounds—insects and frogs, a whippoorwill crying monotonously far away, the dogs moving restlessly behind the house. She did a few slow painful knee bends. Then she took her pocketbook and laundry bag and briefcase and, patting the dogs briefly, went in through the back.

The night-light was on in the kitchen. A few coloring books lay open on the floor, crayons nearby, marbles scattered here and there, a couple of them glowing brilliantly in the dim light. An Oreo cookie had been stepped on and smashed. No one had cleared the remains of dinner off the kitchen table. She looked at the chart on the refrigerator to see who was in charge of dishes. *She* was. She didn't mind the disarray so much as she felt irritated at the food left out. She put the margarine and milk in the refrigerator, noting on two covered casseroles DO NOT TOUCH! signs in her stepdaughter Ruth's tight block printing— probably these were dishes for the fancy dinner she made her father Saturday nights. Lottie closed the refrigerator door quietly.

From the bedroom off the kitchen she could hear the girls' soft breathing. It was hard on her daughter, Lila, to have to

share her room every August when Ruth came, but there was
nothing for it; Ruth, at fourteen, couldn't be put in with the
boys and she couldn't be asked to sleep on the living-room
couch like an overnight guest. It wasn't easy for Ruth, either,
especially since she was meticulous by nature and disdained
Lila's cluttered ways, so much like Lottie's. The only neat part
of the house was Ruth's half of the room, as if a magic circle
had been drawn around it. She even slept neatly and with a
certain style, the sheet smooth up to her neck, her black hair
in one long braid, her pink ballet slippers next to each other
beside the bed. She was thin and dark and angular, on her way
to being tall. Lila at eighteen was taller than either of them: she
was built on a grand scale, like a Viking queen—people told
her she resembled Liv Ullmann, which delighted her. Across
the room she turned in her twisted sheets, mumbling.

When Lottie got to her and Jake's bedroom, Jake was asleep
in his underwear, one arm around Simon, their two-year-old,
the other off the side of the bed. He was snoring softly in the
moonlight. She eased the child out from under him, felt
Simon's diaper, and carried him to his crib. Davy was in bed
with the new baseball glove Jake had given him. These were
her brownish children, a cross between the two of them,
everything burnished, those eyes she could almost see the blue
genes behind, that berry-bright skin. In the bathroom she
brushed her teeth and patted some after-bath splash on herself,
then peed quietly into the toilet bowl full of their pee (at
night they didn't flush so as not to disturb anyone) and closed
the lid.

She eased herself into bed beside Jake—he smelled faintly
of sweat and Simon's baby powder—and snuggled her alcohol-

cooled breasts against his warm back. She licked two of her fingers and massaged her clitoris with them. She put her other hand under the elastic waistband of his shorts. He was moist and soft. Lightly she stroked the hairy skin of his thighs, the corrugated scrotum, the delicate fine skin of his penis. Slowly she felt him bloom, like a night flower.

"Lottie." Half asleep, he turned toward her. "Sweetheart." She kissed his eyelids.

She helped him take off his undershirt and shorts, and dropped them on the floor next to her side of the bed. Sleepily he kissed her throat and her breasts and her belly. Then he lifted himself over her and came into her slowly. She lay on her back running her hands through his thick hair—Davy's already had something of the same texture—and looked up through the skylight at the bright stars.

She woke at eleven in the morning in a sudden flood of rock music, as if the pipes had burst. She ran to the window. Ruth was out in front in her black leotard with a massive radio blaring—she brought the city with her—doing her exercises. Lottie was annoyed at being awakened so sharply, and embarrassed at having this exotic-looking child-woman on the front lawn, her legs in the air, sensual music saturating the area as if they were hosting a block party. "Do it in the back!" Lottie yelled, her head out the window.

After a moment, Lottie thrust her arms out the window as well and waved them around to catch Ruth's attention. The girl seemed not to see her, although she was facing Lottie's way. Lottie rolled the newspaper into a truncheon, then unrolled it. She ripped some pages into pieces and let them drop out the window. They wafted here and there in the warm summer morning, a few coming down a couple of feet from Ruth without seeming to attract her notice. Lottie hollered the girl's name twice and then in a fury took a bottle of hand lotion off the dresser and threw it at the radio. She missed them both.

Ruth turned the radio down but not off. She looked up at Lottie.

"What's the matter with you? Don't you hear me? Don't you see me?"

Ruth shook her head no.

"Turn that off!" Lottie yelled.

Ruth turned it down a little more.

"You didn't see me? I can't believe you didn't see me. I'm right in front of you! I'm dropping newspaper out the window! What did you think it was, snow?"

The girl began doing pliés.

"I'm *talking* to you!"

"I'm *listening* to you. What do I have to do, stand at attention?"

"Show some respect," Lottie said.

"Look, what do you want anyway? I'm doing my exercises."

Lottie took a deep breath. "Just do them in the back. I want you to keep that radio down and do your exercises in the back."

"I'm not going in the back. There's dog shit all over the back."

"Well, use the exercise mat."

"I don't want to. It *smells* back there. And I like the radio loud. Why can't I have it on loud? It's after eleven. What are you going to do, sleep all day?"

Lottie, her head and arms out the window, remembered reading about a French woman who committed suicide by jumping from the roof of the Notre Dame Cathedral; she hit an American tourist who was standing on the ground and both women died.

Lottie took a deep breath and after a moment said in a softer voice, "What's wrong here? What's wrong? Turn the radio off, Ruth, and come into the house. I want to talk to you."

"I don't want to talk to you!" Ruth yelled. "I'm not going into the house! Anyway, it's not a house—it's a shit house!" She turned the music up full blast.

In a rage Lottie saw the station wagon pull into the driveway. Jake waved to her and to Ruth, then went around to help Simon out of the child seat. The dogs leaped out of the open car and Davy climbed over the backseat wearing his baseball glove and went around with Lila to the trunk. Jake threw her the keys and Lila opened the trunk and began lifting out the bags of groceries. As if he were turning a doorknob, Jake made a hand gesture to Ruth to turn the volume down. She continued doing jumping jacks. Slowly, as in a pantomime or a silent movie, the musical score eighties heavy metal at earsplitting volume, all of them, Jake and Lila with the groceries, Simon and Davy dragging a mesh bag of oranges, walked to the middle of the lawn. Ruth began doing pliés.

Jake gestured to Ruth. She waved her arms and pointed up at Lottie. Jake smiled up at Lottie, then turned back to Ruth. He opened his arms to her but she turned away from him and stamped her foot. She pointed up at Lottie again and Lottie could see her face was contorted. Jake leaned over and turned

the radio off, and all at once, as if the sound had suddenly
come back on, or as if Lottie had lost her senses and now in a
single instant had regained them fully, Ruth was standing in
the middle of the lawn stamping her foot in its pink ballet
slipper and screaming in a harsh cracked voice, "I hate her! I
hate her! I hope she drops dead!"

"I only wanted her to turn it down," Lottie said to Jake. He was
sifting flour for waffle batter and Lila was squeezing oranges
with the electric juicer. It made a buzzing sound as she pressed
the oranges against the reamer with the heel of her hand,

Lottie said, "It was on so loud I'm surprised nobody
complained."

He tapped the sifter against the bowl a few times to knock
the flour loose. "Just let her be. She'll come around."

"I can't stand it when she wishes me dead."

"She doesn't mean it."

"She means it."

"Well, everybody wishes everybody dead now and then."

"Oh, Jake, she won't talk to me. She won't look at me."

"That's how she is. She sulks. She does the same with me."

"Well, I can't stand it."

"Well, she knows you can't."

Lottie took a sponge from the sink and began wiping off
the table. "I'll bet she still holds it against me that you're not
with her mother. And she knows it's not my fault."

"She knows and she doesn't know."

"Maybe I ought to have a talk with her."

Lila cut two more oranges in half. "She doesn't look in the
talking mood, if you want my opinion."

"I don't want your opinion."

"What am I supposed to be, a statue?"

Ruth burst in with the pink bottle of hand lotion. "She was throwing things at me," she said. "Do you think it's right of her to throw things at me?"

"I didn't throw that at you! I threw it at the radio! I couldn't get your attention! You wouldn't pay any attention to me!"

"What do you mean, I *wouldn't*? I couldn't hear you! I couldn't see you. I had the sun in my eyes!"

"That's bullshit!" Lottie yelled. "You have a million reasons for everything, but they're all hoked up. Why don't you say there was an eclipse going on so you couldn't see me?"

"Are you calling me a liar? Is that what you're calling me?"

"Yes!" Lottie cried. "That's what I'm calling you!"

"Look, honey, please," Jake began.

They both looked at him.

"My dears, cut it out, both of you. You have to cut it out. Ruth, don't exercise on the front lawn. Do it in the back or go out in the fields. And cut the volume in half. All the cows in the area will miscarry from that stuff."

"What about *her*? You always take *her* side."

"No, I don't," Jake said. "She shouldn't throw things at you."

"I didn't throw it at her! If I wanted to throw it at her, I would have hit her."

"Lottie," Jake had a pleading look in his eye. "I wish you wouldn't throw things at her. And if you didn't throw it at her, then I wish you wouldn't throw things *near* her anymore. If you want Ruth's attention, go down and get it."

"Yeah," Ruth said grinning.

"Don't 'yeah' her," Jake said. "Do you hear me?"

Lila cut four more oranges and pushed them half after half against the reamer. They all listened to the buzz.

"You're cutting too many oranges." Lottie said. "That's enough now."

Lila shrugged but stopped.

They stood in the quiet kitchen.

After a moment Lottie put the sponge back in the sink and dried her hands. She held her right hand out to Ruth. Ruth looked at Lottie. Lottie continued to hold out her hand. Ruth looked down at her feet in their ballet slippers. She pointed a foot, then relaxed it. Without looking at Lottie, she walked past her out the back door.

Lottie showered. Her anger was burnt out and she felt ashamed and sick of it all. She wanted to do exercises in the fields herself. She wanted to light out for the West.

Why did she let Ruth get her goat? Why must she take it personally?

She told herself that the girl's heart had a rent in it and there were many ways to patch a rent. Ruth had patched it with barbed wire: "Why should I? It's not my house." "It's a shame about the broken blood vessels in your thighs." "Do you think *my* breasts will flop at forty?"

And maybe it was true what Lottie told herself but it didn't stop her filling up with wild, vindictive thoughts—lashing out, and then sinking slowly into a slough of shame and depression and remorse.

Once after a weekendful, Lottie woke in the middle of the night with an uneasy feeling in her chest and she asked Jake did he love her and he mumbled in his sleep yes; and she asked him in a small voice did he love her more than anyone else in the world, and he said, yes, there was no one else in the running. Tears ran down her face in the middle of the night as she lay beside her sleeping husband.

During breakfast Lottie tried to act as if bygones were bygones while Ruth answered her in monosyllables. Afterwards Jake got out his flute and Lila her violin and they began playing Telemann's First Canonic Sonata in G Major in the living room. Jake played in his dungarees, barefoot and bare chested in the heat, swaying with his silver flute, eyes half closed, sweat dripping. Lila, in flowery halter and shorts, her hair a bright cloud, her fingernails and toenails newly painted a soft rose color, sat concentrating on the score. She moved the bow of the violin lightly, brightly, as if it were a wand. After a while Ruth noiselessly pushed aside some storybooks and a can of talcum powder to clear a six-foot-square space in front of the players. She found a green ribbon that had been on a box of chocolates one of Jake's pupils had brought him and tied it around her neck. She did a half dozen pliés, then took off in a sweet summery improvisation, as if she were picking flowers and following the flights of bees or birds. As she danced, the pinched disdainful quality left her face and the thin angularity of her body softened. She seemed easier, hardly more than a child dancing to music, given up to it, lost in it and at peace. Davy stood on his chair and waved his arms, conducting as he'd seen the maestro do at Carnegie Hall, where Jake had taken him for his first concert: he was masterly and joyous. Simon, in Lottie's lap, watched Davy and waved his arms in imitation. Davy shot him a dirty look. Slowly Lottie leaned back in her old chair, got her feet up on the hassock, and let the morning's travail recede a bit, come back and recede again, if not be carried wholly out to sea.

She was in the lab a few days later, with a rat in the ether jar, when the phone rang. It was late in the afternoon. "I'll call you back," she told Jake. "Fifteen minutes." Then she added, "I miss you," to soften her abruptness.

The rat ran around the jar frantically. For an instant he stood up on his hind legs, his front paws against the wall of the jar, and looked at Lottie with his weak pink eyes. He took in gulps of the etherized air, ran, stood up, and then dropped. His breathing grew fast and hoarse. She waited two minutes, then lifted the unconscious animal out of the jar and laid him on a paper towel beside the sink. Attached to the cage six inches above the rat was a feeding bottle that had been filled with fixative an hour earlier. Now it was two-thirds empty. A piece of clear plastic tubing was hooked to the neck of the bottle and clamped off there; the other end of the tube reached to the counter. She opened a sterile needle package, then cut through the rat's rib cage with scissors and, holding his heart between her fingers, slipped the needle into the aorta. She hooked the needle to the plastic tube—a little blood backed up—and taped it in place. Then she cut through the auricle, and as the blood oozed out into the sink, opened up the clamp: the fixative, a clear liquid, gushed down the tube. The animal stirred and began to convulse violently, first his upper limbs, then the lower, and finally the tail. After a moment he was still.

Lottie had fixed him alive, arresting all his cells in motion as if she were filming a sports event, a football game, perhaps, and had stopped the film at one particular frame where the players were all moving in different but coordinated directions: this one leaping into the air, that one starting to fall, another blocking for the passer as torn-loose clods of earth flew into their faces but never reached them. She had stopped the rat dead so that her results would be less artifactual in her critics' eyes. Poor creature, he was really all artifact. With his soft white fur and pink eyes he looked like a store-bought Easter bunny. Put him out there on his own with all those streetwise rats and he wouldn't last half an hour. Swiftly and cleanly, she slit the animal's throat, then dissected out the salivary glands. She lifted them gently with the forceps and placed them in the vial of buffer. She unhooked the rat, washed her hands, and called Jake.

"I've got a job for tonight," Jake said. "A choir concert up in Winango. The accompanist took a nap this afternoon and died. An old guy, in his nineties. I played with him once in a group."

"That's lovely. I mean, about the job."

"Well, he was very old. It's two hundred bucks. They're desperate."

"That's okay money." Lottie said. Then she remembered. "What about Ruth? What about the dinner she's making for you?"

"She told me to fuck myself."

Lottie let out a sigh.

"I have to leave now. It's a two-hour drive."

"And Lila's got a date."

"I feel bad about it but I'm not going to turn down two hundred dollars to eat the casserole at its peak."

"Ruth will have to babysit," Lottie said.

Mincing the glands, she had a moment's pleasure thinking about that snotty kid feeding her fancy dinner to a six-year-old and a two-year-old. Ruth had begun to cook when her mother took an expensive course at the Cordon Bleu school in San Francisco, paid for, naturally, by Jake. His ex-wife had not remarried and when she cried to him (collect), Jake's heart bled money. It angered Lottie that he was such a soft touch and they'd had terrible fights about it. But there was no budging him. Behind his stubbornness was his belief that leaving his daughter was the worst thing he'd done in his life. She remembered how bitterly he'd laughed one day when he got a printed request to adopt a fatherless child for an evening a month: "I already have a fatherless child."

Once when they were arguing heatedly, he'd yelled at her, "What about your arrangement with *your* good old ex? How come we never talk about that?"

"What's one thing got to do with the other?"

"It's not relevant that you get a hundred bucks a month when old Charlie remembers? That doesn't affect our finances?"

"You're clouding the issue. You're dragging in extraneous things to take the heat off yourself!"

"A hundred bucks a month for sixteen years! What about inflation?"

"You're just trying to change the subject!" Lottie screamed.

"And he's a professor now and his wife works, too!"

"He's just an associate professor! And his wife's a secretary!" In a shrill voice she reminded him how badly paid academics were in the Southwest and that Charlie had two little children to provide for and a third on the way. She also explained grimly that she'd agreed to such a small amount in the first place because she didn't want any trouble with Charlie all those years when she was on her own—he could have tried to take Lila away.

"Those years are over," Jake said. "The college years are beginning."

"You don't want to help out, you don't have to. We'll get by, we always have."

Jake took a deep breath. "That's a mean thing to say."

After a moment, Lottie apologized. "I just meant she'll probably get a scholarship."

"Like hell, that's what you meant," Jake said. "If she gets one, terrific. And if Charlie kicks in some money, that won't kill anybody either. But Lila will have whatever she needs, regardless. She's my child and you're my wife, whether either of you knows it or not."

"Sorry," Lottie said. "Sorry." She squeezed his hand.

"Still, I wish you'd think over why you can't ask him for anything."

Lottie said she'd think about it, but thinking about it was like fingering a boil. She would have to remember how everything had dried up between her and Charlie, and how she'd abandoned him and taken his daughter away. And although she could hear Jake remonstrating with her in her mind's ear (Don't you think the statute of limitations has run on that? And what's it got to do with Lila's going to college now? And isn't Charlie responsible if Lila's a stranger to him? There were summers, there was Christmas, there were spring vacations), still it didn't quiet her conscience much.

She wondered if she also felt guilty about having Jake and the children and her career. But why should she? She hadn't taken him away from anybody. She hadn't stolen Davy and Simon, plagiarized her Ph.D. thesis. Yet once it crossed her mind to ask Jake if he thought they were paying money for their happiness, for the fact that they genuinely liked each other and the kids and their work, as if such everyday pleasures were wild flukes, random happenings not really in the order of things.

Hours must have gone into that dinner Ruth had prepared, that duck casserole. Of course, Ruth had nothing else to do with her time. The girl had no friends in town because she was never around long enough to make any. And while Lila didn't mind lending Ruth her books, Ruth couldn't sit still. She had her physical life—her dancing, exercising, jogging, swimming in the town pool; her Saturday night cooking feats; and her father.

Did it hurt Ruth, being surrounded by a family that she was part of, but not part of? And when she returned to her mother, did she miss them? Did she want her mother to remarry and have more children? Or was Ruth glad to be free of her father's brood, with all the dirt and noise and competitiveness, and be once more the only child, her mother's focus? Although Lottie had known the girl for seven, almost eight years, it was as if Ruth put on a lead shield in her presence so that she was ignorant of her stepdaughter's inner life.

Did Ruth armor herself because she felt in danger of being drawn to Lottie? One summer Lottie had come upon her old paperback copy of *Great Women in Science*, which she'd had since high school, in the girl's underwear drawer. She also noticed that in family discussions Ruth was especially attentive to whatever Lottie had to say, although in the end, as though catching herself, she would make a derogatory remark. And Lottie was usually missing a scarf or handkerchief in September after Ruth had gone.

As Lottie washed the minced fixed tissue with buffer, she tried not to breathe in too deeply. The fixative, that lethal film, could fix her lungs as well as the rats'. Many of the chemicals she worked with routinely were carcinogens or poisons of other types. She was killing cells in order to have a look at them. At least when she was using osmium she tried to work under a hood, a high-domed chamber with an air vent that sucked off fumes. But the noise was annoying and she felt confined. Occasionally she wondered if she would die of her work. Madame Curie's precious radium had destroyed her blood cells. At least Lottie wasn't working with anything radioactive.

Lottie called home but hung up after one ring. She did another rat. Then she called again and asked Davy, who picked up the phone, to get Ruth.

"If you can wait until eight thirty to serve dinner, I'll come home and eat with you."

After a long pause Ruth said, "Suit yourself."

At seven o'clock she tried to sort out what to take home with her. Having planned to stay at the lab until late Sunday afternoon, she had brought rations as if she were going camping: tuna fish sandwiches for tonight's dinner and peanut butter sandwiches for tomorrow's breakfast, a quart of skim milk, two thermoses of iced tea; Virginia Woolf's *A Room of One's Own*, and the most recent issues of the *Journal of Histochemistry and Cytochemistry* and the *Journal of Anatomy*; also a heavyweight blue wool scarf she was knitting for Lila as part of a hat, scarf, and gloves set for college. In the end Lottie took everything home because, although she would probably return to the lab Sunday morning, she might not, and then the sandwiches would go stale. She set the vials containing the glands minced in buffer in a big bucket of ice, and one of the janitors took it down to the station wagon for her. She put several bottles of alcohol of different strengths, and a large dump jar, on the floor in the back of the car, then packed thick rags between them so that each was cushioned and wedged in tightly.

Although it was not yet dusk, the light was thinning. Lottie double-parked in front of a row of open stores. She bought a cold bottle of Chablis and thought about getting a small bunch of deep-colored rosebuds, tight dark ones that hadn't begun to open yet. She decided not to.

"It's nice of you," Ruth said uneasily. She unwrapped the wine as if it would blow up. Lottie tried not to smile.

Davy and Simon wanted to help Lottie unload the car. She said that she had her lab work with her and they were to keep away from it. "You could get hurt."

"How come you brought it home?" Ruth asked.

Lottie explained that she was halfway through a tissue preparation and that there were different procedures she had to do in a strictly timed sequence, otherwise the tissue would be ruined.

"What kind of tissue?"

"Rat salivary glands."

"Yich," Ruth said. "You kill the rats?"

"You know that."

After a moment Ruth said, "How can you?"

Lottie began explaining her procedures.

"How can you stand it, I mean."

"Oh." Lottie laughed. She thought for a moment. "It's really very complicated. If you want to come to the lab sometime, you're welcome."

"Thanks, but no thanks."

"Where's Lila?"

"Showering upstairs." Ruth was sponging off the table. She looked at Lottie standing by the back door. "You need a hand?"

They carried in the ice bucket together.

After Lottie set up in the downstairs bathroom, she told the boys, "You have to pee or M, you go upstairs. I don't want you in here."

"What's rat sally glands?" Davy asked.

"Salivary glands," Lottie said. "Spit glands. They make spit. You have them, too." She pushed her fingers up at the angles of Davy's lower jaw.

As she closed the door, she saw Davy push his fingers up under Simon's jaw.

Lottie worked in the bathroom with a stopwatch, pipetting the buffer out of the vials and into the dump jar, careful not to touch the tissue. She replaced the buffer with a 30 percent alcohol solution. In the kitchen she could hear Ruth washing dishes. Ruth felt the dishwasher didn't get them clean enough; when she made her special dinners, she didn't want any film on the plates detracting from the taste. Lottie had always assumed Ruth went through this to embarrass her, but if she was washing dishes when Lottie was out of the room, then maybe there was something wrong with her. Maybe she had some washing mania. Was Lottie responsible for this girl or not?

Lila called down, "Ma, can I use your blue eye shadow?"

"What's the matter with yours?" she yelled up, putting her finger on the vial she'd just filled so as not to lose her place.

"Simon put it in the toilet."

"Sure," Lottie screamed. "It's down here. And don't yell from upstairs."

Lila wore a cherry-red sleeveless blouse and a ruffled skirt that tied in back at the waist. Her skin was pink from the shower. She had on gold hoop earrings and Lottie's white sandals. She was fuller than Lottie had been at her age. She was coming into her own time, like a bright bloom of some promising new strain.

"Can I wear the sandals?"

"You're wearing them."

"Do you mind?"

"Not much. They look better on you than on me."

"Oh, Ma."

"Truth is truth. Even your feet are beautiful."

"Oh, Ma. Just tell me where the eye shadow is. Why don't you wear gloves? That stuff can't be good for your hands."

"They're clumsy, gloves."

"How can they be clumsy? Surgeons wear them."

"You really look lovely."

"Oh, Ma."

Lila put her pinkie into the pot of pale-blue eye cream, traced a soft shadow over her lid and up toward the outer tip of her blond eyebrow. Lottie watched her daughter as if she were doing something of extraordinary interest. Often she found herself caught in this way, looking on with intense absorption as one of her children did a routine thing.

"Ma, what is this stuff? It stinks. And your eyes are tearing." They looked at each other in the mirror. "Don't touch yourself," Lila said. With a piece of tissue paper she wiped her mother's eyes.

The doorbell rang.

"I got it! I got it!" Davy yelled.

"Go talk to him, Ma, would you? I'll be a minute."

Lottie pipetted alcohol into the last two vials and wrote down the time. Then she washed her hands and patted her eyes with cool water. In the kitchen she asked Ruth if it would be all right to offer Ted, Lila's boyfriend, a glass of the wine Lottie'd brought home.

"Suit yourself," Ruth said.

It took Lottie a few minutes to find the corkscrew. It was at the bottom of a shelf of utensils they rarely used, beneath a set of pastry brushes, a small pasta machine, a cork you could recork champagne with; most of these were presents from her first wedding. Lottie went into the living room to shake hands with Ted.

"Hi, Mrs. Hart. Nice to see you."

He always called her Mrs. Hart. Davy had corrected him several times but it didn't stick. Lottie had explained that it was Lila's last name, not hers, but she really didn't care one way or the other. Davy cared and every time Ted called her Mrs. Hart, Davy would frown or cough or stamp his foot. This evening he threw his head back repeatedly as if he had hair in his eyes, then offered Ted his hand. Ted bent down and shook it.

Holding out his hand, Simon toddled over after Davy.

"You remember my daughter Ruth," Lottie said.

"Stepdaughter," Ruth corrected. "Would you like a glass of wine?" She had the bottle in her hand.

"Sure, thanks. Let me open it for you."

"Oh, that would be wonderful!" Ruth said, beaming.

"Yeah, sure," Ted nodded.

Simon said, "Wonderful!" and toddled into the kitchen after Ruth.

"Well," Lottie said, amused. "Thanks."

"Oh, it's nothing," Ted smiled. He seemed about ten feet tall and he had his shirt open to the fourth button, two silver chains around his neck. His skin was red from the sun and he had a few blond, almost white hairs on his chest. He was a nice-looking boy, on the basketball team and in the honor society (Lila had told her about him with pride). There was something good-natured and easy in the way he treated Davy and Simon.

Lottie wondered if Ted resembled Lila's father but she could no longer remember what Charlie had looked like in high school. The Charlie of her mind's eye was on the football field at the end of college or in bed watching TV at the end of their marriage. He was always massive, even in depression.

Lottie and Ted stood sipping wine and making small talk while Ruth did ballet exercises, occasionally touching Ted's knee with a toe. After what seemed a long time, Lila came out, apologetic and radiant. Ted reddened, both his face and his chest. Lottie resisted the impulse to look at his crotch. She

waved from the door as he helped Lila into the front seat of his
father's pickup truck.

Ruth had laid the table with a white cloth and napkins, a
bouquet of wildflowers—yellow buttercups and honeysuckle
and dog roses—in a crystal vase in the center. At either side of
the flowers she had lit a long white candle, despite the warmth
of the night. The candles drew attention away from Davy's baseball glove on the floor under his chair and one of Lila's big lacy
bras hanging over a basket of unfolded laundry, and focused it
instead on the fresh flowers, the wine bottle, which Ruth had
set in a glass bowl filled with ice, the name cards she'd put at
each setting (an unnecessary act since each of them sat in the
accustomed place). The glasses and the silverware shone, even
in the candlelight, and Lottie wondered if maybe that was
what Ruth had been scrubbing—the glasses, the silverware. Or
perhaps the silver candlesticks. These new possibilities cheered
her. The glass of wine had gone to her head and she was feeling
pleased with herself for having made the pain-in-the-ass trip
home.

"Oh, it's so elegant," she said to Ruth. And that silly phrase
went on booming through her brain for hours afterwards, as if
it had great import, as if it were the last sound anyone would
hear and needed urgently to be decoded, emphasized properly,
absorbed.

She remembered the scene as if they were fixed: Ruth coming toward them, a silver tureen (wedding gift from Charlie's
aunt) of vichyssoise in her hands; Davy reaching over to touch
one of the buttercups; Lottie standing behind her chair survey-
ing the table with a sense of well-being. "Oh, it's so elegant."

Immediately after she spoke, they all heard the terrible sound of some substantial thing crashing and shattering. She was at the bathroom door at once, or else Simon was there and then she was there. He was standing at the door of the bathroom looking dazed, his hair wet, alcohol dripping down the sides of his face. She thought it was dripping down the sides of his face, down the temples, down near the earlobes. The dump jar was in shards on the floor.

She grabbed a handful of napkins and mopped at his forehead.

"Did you get it in your eyes?"

She carried him into the bathroom and turned on the shower full force. As he wriggled and screamed, she held him faceup under the cold water.

"Did it go in your eyes?"

He was sobbing.

"Did you swallow it? Did you drink it?" She began to shake him.

By now he was wet through to the skin and shivering despite the warmth of the evening. Coughing, gasping, Simon tried to turn his face out of the way of the oncoming cold water but Lottie held him tight.

"Mama, you're drowning him!" Davy cried in an anguished voice.

Lottie yelled to Ruth, "Call the rescue squad! The number's on the wall, next to the telephone."

"Mama! Mama!"

"You get out of here!" Lottie yelled at Davy. "There's no room! There's glass all over the floor!"

Davy began to cry.

"Shut up!" she said. "For God's sake, shut up!" She could hardly hear herself over the boom in her brain.

They spent the night in the hospital, Lottie walking back and forth between the emergency room where they were observing Simon and the fluorescent-lit waiting room, where Ruth and Davy sat propped up against each other, asleep. A drunk who was also waiting was having a loud argument, although he was alone. One of the overhead lights was broken and flickered on and off.

The pediatrician, who looked to be six months pregnant, had been very crisp with Lottie, although perhaps that was her way. When she took Simon into an examining room, she seemed reluctant to have Lottie follow her.

Half an hour later an administrator came out and asked Lottie a series of questions, writing the answers on a printed form. Had this child ever had an accident before? Had he been in the hospital before for any reason? Had the other children had accidents? He looked at Ruth and Davy.

"What do you take me for?" Lottie asked sharply.

The man seemed surprised. "I ask everybody the same questions. They're on the form."

Lila and Ted showed up at one, smelling faintly of beer. Lottie noticed that Lila's red blouse was misbuttoned.

At three in the morning Jake came in wearing his tuxedo, his face tight. He hurried past her into the emergency room.

Lottie stood apart. The light flickered on and off in the harshly lit room and after a while she closed her eyes. She wished she could close her ears. She kept hearing the phrase, "Oh, it's so elegant," with the emphasis now on this syllable, now on that, as if it were coming out a megaphone, as if it were the only thing real. How long she stood she didn't know. She wasn't sleepy but she felt very odd and strained, as if she hadn't been to bed for days. She waited although she forgot for what.

When Jake came back, he touched her cheek.

"He's sleeping," Jake said. "He looks all right to me."

"Who knows," Lottie said.

The next few days she stayed home and stood guard over Simon. Were his steps slurred? Was he bumping into things? She watched him as he ate, looking for signs of gagging or vomiting. She asked him about double vision but she could not make him understand. Usually eager for her attention, Simon seemed uncomfortable with her worried shadowing of him. He avoided her. Lottie could not stop herself. She continued to be hounded by that vapid phrase, "It's so elegant," and occasionally she would see it—cut in granite, as if on a gravestone.

Although Simon never showed any ill effects from the accident, Lottie continued to feel grim. If only she hadn't come home. Jake said coming home was a gracious act. He reminded her that she had gone a few months earlier to the emergency room with a neighbor whose two-year-old son had eaten the shiny black berries of a deadly nightshade plant and had to have his stomach pumped. And hadn't she choked on something herself, Jake asked her, and nearly drowned when she was a girl? She called her parents and had an uncharacteristically long conversation with her mother, although Lottie never mentioned Simon except to say that they were all fine.

She went to work and finished her experiment and sent in the results, but she got little pleasure from proving herself right and the journal's referees wrong. And her sleep was disturbed by nightmares. In a recurrent one she was exposed to radiation from a leak in her lab and lost all her hair and her vision. She wore a purple Afro wig and mirrorlike sunglasses. Behind them her eyes were gone, replaced by two of the boys' bright marbles: one agate, one cat's-eye. She would wake shuddering and Jake would hold her until she quieted. Although he counseled patience, she could not imagine ever being herself again.

Just before Labor Day the editor phoned to tell her off the record that her revised paper would be accepted. She did feel vindicated—not a bad feeling. She knew she would feel expansive when she received the referees' crow-eating reports. Jake said they should celebrate now as well as later and so the six of them piled into the car and went to Randy's Grill for cheeseburgers and milk shakes.

Afterwards Jake wanted to take a walk in the marshes. Lila had planned to sort out her books and wall hangings that evening—in a week she was entering Swarthmore (not so far away, her mother told herself)—but agreed to go along "for old times' sake." They put on their galoshes and rubbed their hands and faces with mosquito repellant. The dogs could hardly stand still as they waited for Lottie to unlatch the gate to the backyard; they whimpered in ecstasy.

It had been a hot day but there was a slight breeze now and it was pleasant to walk through the cool, dank marsh. The flashlights Jake had brought in the backpack were unnecessary

because the sky was drenched with stars. Ruth was walking on the far side of her father, a little apart. It occurred to Lottie that she would always be there, a little apart. Lottie looked away.

Jake and Lila were trying to explain something to Davy. Simon tugged at Lottie's hand because he wanted to hear, too, and for a moment she held him, then let him tug free.

Jake held a tube of rolled-up star charts which he was waving for emphasis. Davy was pointing up at the milky sky and Jake was shaking his head. "Nobody knows that. By the time the light reaches us, the star may have changed or disappeared or exploded even. Something may have happened."

It didn't make sense to Davy.

"It's like a photograph of someone taken years ago." Jake handed the star charts to Ruth and took his wallet out of his pocket. He got a flashlight from his backpack.

"There's you at six months. Would you recognize yourself? It's nothing like you now."

Davy said his hair was still the same color.

Jake sighed. "Here's my father, your grandfather. He's dead twenty years, may he rest in peace. He looks fine in the picture, doesn't he?"

Davy said querulously that he didn't understand.

Jake flipped to another picture. "Look, there's your mother, way before any of us knew her." He shone the flashlight on an old photograph that was torn in several places and then repaired with tape that had yellowed and contracted so that the various parts of the picture were no longer exactly aligned. It was Lottie standing in front of her parents' house in a light summer dress her grandmother had made for her; her head was markedly cocked.

She wondered if she had taken this uncharacteristically awkward position deliberately, for some reason she could no longer remember, or whether she was simply self-conscious at the time about being photographed; it was also possible that the inclination of her head had resulted from the tape's having shrunk.

"How old are you here, Lottie? Eight? Ten?"

Lottie watched Jake and Davy examine the photograph. Davy was upset—Davy, who was younger and smaller than the girl in the photograph. She longed to comfort him, to explain the stars and herself to him, to be able to tell him that even when she eventually disappeared, like the stars, she would still be his mother for all time.

She took the photograph from Jake and held her flashlight to it. She was still obviously a child, but how old she couldn't say. As she looked at the pale face and thin arms and legs, the still undeveloped and slightly asymmetrical child's body, a dreadful feeling came over her in the bright marsh, of discon- nectedness, as if she were herself some strange taped-together creature, the likes of which had never been seen before.

NOTHING HUMAN

"D EAR," SHE CALLS out. "Did you wash your hands
after you peed or whatever you did in the bathroom?"
It is four o'clock in the morning. She is lying on her back
in the double bed in their dark cabin on the *AmaDolce* cruise
ship on the Main River, or the Rhine River, or the Moselle,
they all feed into each other anyway. With her husband she
is on a tour of romantic castles and medieval towns, most of
them meticulously reconstructed after World War II. Bamberg
and Würzburg and Miltenberg and Rothenburg . . .

Barefoot, without his contacts in, he is inching his way back
to bed, one hand moving crabwise along the wall that sepa-
rates the bathroom from the bedroom, the other hand—he is
bending forward—feeling over the bedclothes for the pillow.
He is a very tall, bulky man, and the tight quarters and the
blackness—they cannot see each other—make him uneasy.

By the movements of the mattress, she feels him enter the
bed: a mild wave rolls under her as if they are not on a ninety-
three-thousand-ton cruise ship but on a raft.

"I never wash my hands in the middle of the night," he
whispers.

"You don't? Really? Why not?"

He adjusts the pillow, brings the sheet and cover up to his chin. "I don't want to wake myself up."

They speak as if they are in different time zones, he whispering, she talking in a high-pitched, brittle voice. "But you're up! You woke *me* up! What is all this sotto voce stuff? Why not just wash your hands?"

"Sorry! I'm trying to be quiet."

"Well, washing your hands doesn't make any more noise than peeing—or whatever you did."

"*Peed*, that's what I did . . . if you must know."

"I didn't ask what you did. Why didn't you wash your hands, *that's* what I asked you. We went over this years and years ago, and you said you understood and you got it and you promised!" She rises on her elbows, sliding her head up along the wall. Her hair is dyed a dark chestnut color with "warm" highlights, her "natural" color, more or less. She is a small, fine-boned woman, slender, agile. In her fantasies, she can still be mistaken for the feisty forward she was forty-five years earlier on the Bryn Mawr women's soccer team.

"Not at night. I can't recall the conversation exactly but I never would have said I'd wash my hands at night. During the day, it's arguable. But at night, sometimes I get up three, four times during the night, I'm not washing my hands. It interferes with the flow." He feels a breeze. Maybe she has tossed her half of the blanket in his direction? "Hey, what're you doing? Are you hot or something?" He hears or imagines he hears an exasperated sigh. "Where you going?"

In her peach-colored shortie nightgown, she makes her way gingerly around the foot of the bed, holding out her small flashlight, which projects a soft white tire of light. Because of the flashlight and her bantam weight, she has an easier time getting around the cabin than he does. As soon as they first entered it, he seemed like Alice when she's ten feet tall. The cruise manager told them there were no larger accommodations: this is a one-size-fits-all ship.

Democratic, she told the manager.

Procrustean, her husband said, after they left the manager's office.

At the moment, she finds herself relishing the rare tactical advantage, although she is confused by the feeling: she loves this man; their marriage is not ordinarily a battle. Why is she being so bitchy?

"Where you going?" he repeats. He demands.

"Where do you *think* I'm going? Out for a swim?"

Inside the bathroom, she does not turn on the overhead light—too bright—but instead sets the flashlight sideways on the metal sink. In the semidark, she drops the toilet seat, which he has left standing (the water looks dark, so probably he *was* peeing), and drops the toilet seat lid as well—why risk dispersing any noxious microorganisms up into the air when she flushes? And she *will* flush; just now, she does not feel like peeing into his pee. (Although the tainted water is a love gift: he doesn't flush during the night so as not to wake her.) She flushes vehemently, then jiggles the handle several times—and when the sound of water stops, flushes again. After which she sits down and pees. Flushes. In the faint light, she washes her hands for the exemplary twenty seconds, maybe twenty-five.

When she opens the bathroom door, he is snoring.

"For God's sake, put on your CPAP machine!"

There is a momentary pause, then he continues snoring.

Scanning with her flashlight, she makes her way past the mahogany-veneered built-in closet and drawers, the small strip of desk, atop which is the large computer/television screen—which she can't quite figure out how to use. He somehow easily manages to get live pictures of the water in front of them as the ship moves and also of other boats coming at them; and porn, he gets that as well, with sound. The sound is the important part, he says.

It occurs to her now that he couldn't have been whacking off in the bathroom. He is more comfortable doing it sitting down, and even if he were standing up facing the wall, say, with his iPad placed on the toilet tank, he needs sound. Those ecstatic female gasps, sobs, screeches—he cannot come without them. Although, thank God, he doesn't need them in real life: she happens to be a quiet comer. And those dramatic shrieks certainly would have awakened her.

And he is a considerate man.

And an honest one: if he *had* been jerking off, and she asked him, he would have told her.

Could it really have been his peeing that woke her? And then she was lying there waiting to see if he would wash his hands. Lying in wait. What is going on with her?

Maybe she woke on her own, with a sense of tension.

From a dream?

She vaguely remembers something . . . about dogs. Or rodents. Dog-rodents. Was she being chased? By German shepherds. With rat faces and long sharp incisors. Yes?

At the window she pulls back the heavy brocade outer curtain, and then the gauzy inner "privacy" curtain. There is no moon. Only black water and, at a little distance, the shore. Maybe she imagines the shore. At least there looks to be some banked-up area. Between towns there are long stretches of riverbank. She feels momentarily apprehensive, imagines herself a shadow running beside that black water looking for a thicket of trees, a hole in the ground, a pigsty—any place to hide.

Not the cruise she had wanted—she would have preferred Basel to Amsterdam, with the small romantic towns and castles brief interludes. But they had been nervous about going to Germany, and so had put off making arrangements until only the Nuremberg–Trier cruise was left. *She* had put off making arrangements. He has never been an adventurous traveler, prefers summering in the Berkshires, which he always did with his late wife. A physicist, he is at home in starry space, and with invisible particles and waves, but he can't bear getting lost on the road, especially in a foreign country. Why can't everyone speak English?

And so when they travel, she occasionally books them on tours, where the chance of anything out of the way befalling them is small. She is not a fan of tours. Feels chaperoned.

She can remember only once going on a tour before she met him. It was to visit medical facilities in Costa Rica, with her first husband, whom she'd met in the Peace Corps in rural South Korea. She was teaching English and some Spanish and learning Korean—she loved languages, still does, not only tracking down the tangled roots of words, but also exploring the dark cave of her mouth, finding the strange places she has to put her tongue to get the sounds right. He was purifying drinking water and trying out different methods of irrigation.

So young, what were they? Twenty-three. They'd married in a traditional Korean ceremony, 결혼식, a *gyeolhon*, and then, back in the States, had a Jewish wedding. Became physicians together, did residencies in pediatrics, and worked for the "underserved" in New York City. Summers they'd spent practicing in Nepal, Yemen, Mali, Botswana, Nicaragua—schlepping their two daughters with them. It had been the life her husband and she had wanted, useful and, now and again, thrilling.

While she is not up for roughing it any longer, she is not exactly ready to watch summer stock either; she wants at least to *see* the world; and once they arrive at wherever her second husband has agreed to let her take him—northern Spain, Sicily, Turkey, even China and Hanoi (each year they have gone on at least one trip and they have been married ten years) he is usually pleased. They are both pleased. They are especially easy and loving—even romantic—on vacations.

But this vacation feels different. Gutenberg's original printing press, the Chagall windows, blah-blah . . . He was impatient even about the thirteen Nobel Prize winners, most of them in physics, from Würzburg; didn't look up any of them on his iPhone, which, she teases, is practically sutured to his fingers. He just drummed his fists against his thighs in Würzberg as the local guide proudly rambled on. Didn't ask a question, her husband, who usually asks good questions, honest questions; he is not the type who speaks to impress his fellows, or to trip up the guide.

It is a fine second marriage. She has reliable taste in husbands. Although he lacks her first husband's pizzazz, this husband is patient and distinguished. As chief scientist, age twenty-eight, in the Kennedy administration, he showed that Russian missile production was verifiable through satellite photography: international treaties became possible. Now he figures out how to conserve energy heating New York City apartments, and he teaches about the physics of climate change, and some of the time still lectures about leptons and gauge bosons and hadrons, words she finds fetching. He is busy, busy, busy.

Yet he can almost always be interrupted. The grandchildren call—"Google" him, as he puts it—when they are writing physics or chemistry papers. Her daughters want his take on things—he is a sensible, approachable stepfather; his many children call, students call, administrators call. And he is almost always even tempered, sweet; yells rarely, mostly at Windows, only very occasionally at her.

Oh, she had more in common with her first husband—not just medicine but also they read novels together; this husband doesn't like to get lost even in a novel. And body type—her first husband had been a gymnast as a kid, and had remained wiry and lithe. And he made stick figures out of tongue depressors with balloon breasts, or deflated balloon dicks—that would get his child patients laughing, get *her* laughing. Although he could grow gloomy, now and then, dark ... That husband would have fit comfortably into this cabin. She feels sad, a wash of nostalgia floods her, but he has been dead a long time, her first husband, and she is on good terms with him in her mind; she dreams of him still, maybe once a month—it is like a little visit.

But there is no doubt that she and this cheerful, equable husband are, now, on edge. As she stands uneasily straining to see out the cabin window, his snoring, which usually drives her crazy—besides keeping her awake, it indicates he is struggling to take in air—is oddly comforting. The dense, nasal sounds; the implication of well-fed-ness, for snoring is often a disease of the overweight, and he could stand to lose ten pounds; the human creaturely noisiness—he is alive! Alive! This bugling of his affords her a transient sense of calm as she looks out the black window. His trumpeting seems almost to assert the presence of nearby troops, "our" troops.

She closes the curtains. Gets into bed and feels for him, feels him—wild thin hedge of hair around his balding head; seamed, cross-stitched neck. He is sleeping on his side, facing away from her. He stays sleeping while she massages his back through the royal blue pajamas she bought him for the trip. She relishes the warmth given off by his flesh in the thick air-conditioning of the cabin, considers slipping her hand beneath the waistband of his pajama bottoms to grow his dick. (But he needs his sleep.)

After her first husband died, she feared she'd never see an erection again—oh, a *cherished* erection. And then she met him and fell wildly (and with trembling relief) in love. They'd been reckless before they married, teenager-ish, gone at it whenever either of their apartments didn't have a kid in it: "Gotta free crib," one would phone, giggly, mimicking their teenage children, to alert the other, who'd hotfoot it over. They'd found sweets they thought they'd never taste again, they were furtive children hiding from their children. She slunk around, fearing she was cuckolding her dead husband. In a dream he lay at the foot of their bed . . .

More than a decade ago . . .

After a while she says, "Put it on, dear. The CPAP machine. It's bad for you to sleep without it."

"Huh?"

She pummels his back gently with her small fists. "You are snorting and hawing and braying."

"What're you talking about?" His speech is sleep slurred. "I'm not even asleep."

"Well, you're awake snoring then. Put it on. Without that machine—I've told you this, goddamnit!—without that CPAP, you're thirty percent more likely to have a heart attack or stroke. Those little mammillary bodies on either side of the hypothalamus . . . they show withering on autopsy in people with sleep apnea, just like with alcoholics . . . memory, intellect, gone. Poof!" She slaps one hand against the other and brings them both up over her head, as if she were playing cymbals.

"Hah?" He rolls over to face her—he is semi-awake. Although he cannot see her, he fumbles for her hands—once he finds any part of her, nothing about her is ever far away—murmurs, "I'm an adult, not one of your kid patients, let me be . . ."

But he likes that she cares, looks after him, even if not always in the gentlest manner. And she seems proud of him, maybe even considers him a bit of a trophy husband, paunch and all: he grins in the dark. Kisses one of her hands, then the other, and feels the urge to lick deeply around the insides of her palms, round and round; but checks himself, he doesn't know why, releases her. Turns away and reaches for the gray plastic box that encases the positive pressure machine, feels here and there over its smoothness until he detects the slight indentation of the on/off strip, depresses it hard: it lights up fluorescent green, and with a great whooshing sound, air begins to flow out of the tubing. He gets the black straps over his fore-head and cheeks so that the clear plastic triangular mask attached to the hose fits snugly over his nose and mouth.

It is unpleasant going to sleep wearing all this paraphernalia; his nose is chronically congested, which makes breathing through the mask difficult. And he worries, absurdly, that he appears to be engaged in S&M practices. When he puts on the CPAP machine, he has to pull straps over his head to keep the mask in place; and then the mask sticks out, to say nothing of the long, thick tubing. Conjures up porn he's seen on the Internet—men in masks, with leather straps . . .

He's a little embarrassed about her divining or ferreting out of him whatever mildly perverse sexual appetites (curiosities, really) he didn't know he had. And then she wants to enact everything with him, for him, satisfy him, although he supposes that is a good thing in a wife. And she has her own little kinky businesses she has always been upfront about—a hard twist on a nipple helps her come, or a bit of finger up her ass. Turns out he likes some pulling on his scrotum, or having her lick him in certain places, and sometimes he likes to bite *her* behind, nibble it. Not important, he can certainly do without these things.

Why do without them, she says.

His previous wives had adapted to his snoring. Well, he didn't remember how the first one adapted, they never talked much, not clear why he married her—afraid of women? She looked like his mother? Ended in divorce, after three kids, twenty years.

The second one used earplugs and spent an occasional night on the living room couch, that was another twenty-year marriage. She actually snored a bit herself. Lightly. Which didn't bother him, meant she was no insomniac. A more placid type than this wife; trained as a lawyer, but worked as an arbitrator, above the fray. And she was a brilliant cook, turned out a new dish most evenings without a recipe, scrumptious, especially her pasta sauces, he was skinny back then, she tended toward overweight—more than tended. But what nice big brown eyes! And a devoted mother to their children, although the younger, their son, fought with her about everything and nothing. And a good storyteller, his wife was, even if some of the stories turned out to be apocryphal, and she repeated herself. What wife doesn't repeat herself? What husband?

Murdered. By a hit-and-run driver. Plowed down. Never found the bastard. Guy must have been blind-drunk because she was a big bright woman in a red suit crossing Riverside Drive on a summer morning, carrying her aluminum briefcase plastered with photos of him and the children.

Truth is, he can't remember much about her. He had loved her dearly but can't recall the sex, the arguments (he liked to think they didn't argue, but that can't be), the texture of their life together.

His new wife had objected to his snoring and insisted he see a doctor. So his sleep apnea got diagnosed, which he supposes is a good thing, although he seems to have developed atherosclerosis high blood pressure lipids despite CPAP and echo stress tests, all the fancy expensive medical care she gets for him. Sometimes he thinks he has whatever he has—if he has anything, since he feels just fine, plays doubles tennis twice a week—*because* of all the medical care she gets for him.

She has a lot of zest herself, which he appreciates, but she is always trying to get to the bottom of things, which is pesty:

wants to know why he can't remember the texture of life between him and his dead wife. His dead beloved wife is dead, that's why. But the current beloved wife believes it has a meaning. Or meanings. This wife feels the issue is psychological, thinks she has deep psychological insights—she points out that he cannot remember his mother either, and he supposedly adored his mother—and wants him to see a shrink. She saw one after her first husband died.

But he is almost always happy, it is his nature, the overexamined life is not for him. CPAP yes; psychiatrist, no. There is nothing wrong with his brain—his curriculum vitae is quite a few pages long. True, when he got to graduate school and heard lectures by the likes of Feynman, Schwinger, and Gell-Mann, he realized he wasn't Nobel Prize material. Those guys, Feynman especially, came up with things he could hardly understand, let alone concoct—*physici-gicians!* Yet the way he's used his brains, his good head—for disarmament, against climate change: he would do it again. Nutty idea, that he needs a psychiatrist. Reassured, he feels himself subside, sink back into an even, heavy sleep.

She lies listening. With her flashlight she checks her watch. Four thirty. She turns her head from side to side, hears the crackling. It is as if she has paper that crinkles in her neck, tissue paper. Doesn't hurt, thank heavens, but it is odd hearing sounds emanating from her neck, as if it needs oil. *She* needs oil. Will she really get up at seven A.M. and go down to breakfast, eat too much smoked salmon and horseradish on small effete goyish bagels and then scramble to join up with her fellow tourists in the red group or the green group or the yellow group? (But not the blue group—the "gentle" group. She is old enough for that, but too fit, too trim, still 104 pounds, and springy as a little terrier.)

As he sleeps on, and the machine soughs, or more likely he is soughing—the mask probably doesn't fit tightly enough and, she swears, lowing sounds occasionally escape him—she moves an arm up beside her head and raises and turns down her toes. Supinates and pronates. Feet and hands. Why is she so restless, so fidgety? And will she really join the others in a few short hours wearing in her ear the little headset the ship provides so that each passenger can hear her or his own local guide for the red group, the green, etc. They will ride in different buses with color-coded signs on the dashboard, ride up, up to the high castle with a bear's head with yellow eyes mounted on a dark inner wall, the heavy wooden table and chairs in the dining room, the small gabled windows looking down, down on the brilliant blue Main or Rhine or the Moselle, the lush, ordered green fields beyond. As if peace and plenty had reigned here forever . . . Back in town, the guide will joke as they walk: "Men, hold on to your wallets, for sure your wife will want to buy this lovely dirndl or that crystal vase"—as if it is *Mad Men* time or medieval times, the men in charge of everything. Evidently Angela Merkel's having assumed the chancellorship has not yet trickled down to these small medieval towns.

Nor has the murder of the European Jews. Or if it has, no one talks about it. During the week they've been here, only one guide, a balding fellow in leather lederhosen, has mentioned the word "Jew." He walked his group of tourists through Bamberg, told them there used to exist hundreds of

years ago "hop Jews," Jews who grew and harvested hops, used
in brewing beer to give a bitter flavor, and also as a mild ster-
ilant. Unlike many Germans, he spoke an awkward English.
Outside a pub/restaurant he gestured toward a six-pointed
star on a sign over the door, and asked the group, "Any idea
what means this?"

A short American man answered, perhaps hopefully, "Jews
are welcome here?"

The guide shook his head, explained that the symbol
originated in the Middle Ages, stood for fire and water, necessary to make beer. This pub has fire and water, and so the sign
means, "Beer is ready now." At the end of the tour, she asked
what happened to the descendants of the hop Jews, the Jews
of Bamberg, during the Second World War. The tour guide
turned off his mike. And told her only one Jew survived the
war. The town was cleansed of Jews, cleaned of Jews, cleared
of them all. He gave her directions to the new synagogue, built
in the last few years by Russian Jews who had recently immi-
grated, and to a monument to the murdered Jews, near the
synagogue. She and her husband managed to find their way.
Construction going on, with loud noises of drills and laying of
pipes. The monument was covered, but to protect it, not to
hide it, and the new synagogue was closed—it was the middle
of a weekday—so they could not enter.

But this was encouraging.

Although, why did the guide turn off his mike when he
talked about the fate of those Bamberg Jews?

Well, it is depressing. Who wants to talk about something
depressing? And especially to a group of tourists on vacation.

But listing the percentage of the town destroyed by

"bombing" is also depressing; yet that guide and, come to think of it, almost every guide, offered that number right up close to the beginning of her/his talk.

Perhaps he was ashamed of what his people had done and so didn't want anyone to hear, to remember. Many Jews were, are also ashamed. "It looks as though we have no merit at all, otherwise so many troubles could not have befallen us." She'd read that in the diary of a Jewish teenager who was deported from Brussels and murdered in Auschwitz.

Or is it that the guide believed the others wouldn't be interested, that the Holocaust was a niche event, of concern only to a relative few—only to Jews themselves. And perhaps that is true: except for that short American man trying to decipher the sign outside the pub, no one has asked a question about the Jews.

Or maybe it is an out-of-date concern, unfashionable, shows her age, like wearing one of those fox pelts around your neck with feet attached and full face, teeth . . . One of her husband's children, the youngest, said, when she mentioned her unease about the trip, "Oh, that's ancient history, the murder of the Jews, Berlin is the swingingest city on the planet. Think about Bosnia and Herzegovina, Darfur. In the Congo civil war, both sides killed and ate the Pygmies." Dreadful, she agreed. Told him they send money to Darfur, that there are more Jews in the Save Darfur movement than Sudanese. She did not want to argue with her stepson; he is, after all, her stepson; and his mother she heard had no luck arguing with him and she was a lawyer. She did not do the math to show that all the other genocides put together . . . No, she refused to enter the genocide contest, that is really yesterday's news, refrained even from saying that the language of her grandparents is dead, murdered. Who cares about the death of a language? Of a culture. A branch of her grandmother's family was murdered, too. She doesn't even know their names. Dim memory of her grandmother knitting and crying in her parents' home in New Jersey.

Or maybe there was some other reason he turned off the mike.

After each of the next few little daily tours, each with new local guides, where no mention was made—the talks were Jew-clean (although rubble share was quoted daily as if it were the Dow Jones Industrial Average)—she spoke. It cost her to speak: fullness in the throat and ears. It also would have cost her not to speak. At the end of each spiel, she asked the guide what had happened to the Yuden from this little town, Miltenberg or Spielsburg or Pestburg, in the Second World War. Always she was answered off mike. But then, it must be said, she asked at the end of the spiel, after the end—she asked privately. She did not want to call too much attention to herself, single herself out as different. She did not want to sew a yellow star to her chest. One memorable response, a happy if breezy one by a plump guide in her sixties, was, "Oh, we warned them and they all escaped." Miltenberg was the town. She was surprised. She was so, so pleased, she was almost tearful. If true, this should be known more widely, should be reported to Yad Vashem. While not Le Chambon-sur-Lignon, the near-legendary town in southern France where the descendants of French Huguenots hid three to five thousand Jews and a few others—German deserters—in their homes throughout the war, still, little brave Miltenberg was worthy of mention. She double-checked with a knot of guides chatting in German and they all stopped speaking. Finally, one, a woman in her fifties, said, mournfully, in English, "I don't know who told you that. Every Jew was killed. I am so ashamed."

She herself felt dreadful, as if her people had been killed again just now right in front of her while she stood by doing nothing. And then she felt foolish for having been taken in. But after a while, she was appreciative: this other guide was ashamed. She liked her, did not like the limber guide in Nuremberg, an ex-dancer, also in her fifties, who said, "The Jews? I wasn't born then. And my mother was a child. My father was sent to the eastern front, didn't even know where he was going. Lost a leg there. He was only sixteen." She had nodded vigorously at that dancer/guide, and smiled, and her husband had smiled and the guide smiled as they toured the vast Nuremberg parade grounds where hundreds of thousands of Nazis had smiled, beamed, as they listened, rapt, to Hitler.

Five A.M. She remains wide awake. His machine breathes obstreperously. Should she wake him and ask that he take off the mask for a minute? She wants to embrace him. She feels forlorn. In the dark, she clutches at her genitals through her nightgown.

They have not made love since they started the cruise. A week ago. And she was too rushed and tense the week before, getting ready.

Not that frequency matters, so long as they care about each other; and making love helps them care about each other, although, since they started having to schedule it in, it has become a little like brushing and flossing, something almost hygienic, good for you. Yet there is passion in it, too, it erupts right out of the schedule. You do it with regularity to show you are a human being, that you are alive and civilized and can still become ecstatic. You can still do it. You still *want* to do it. And it is, after all, a sign of love; and the repetition of it, the making of it into a weekly habit, like phoning their children and speaking to the grandchildren—they have an enormous number of grandchildren (she has three, twin boys, age five, and a two-year-old girl, and he has four older ones and three little ones and she is on good terms with them all, although of course her own are her own)—those phone calls solidify her, connect her to other human beings, to the human world. On this ever-moving boat on this German river she receives on her smartphone twelve-second videos entitled "Abe turns over," "Lucas 'reads,'" "Sara takes bath with new labradoodle puppy named Sherbert" (well, the last is a little much for her sense of sanitary boundaries, but she emails back to her daughter, simply, "Wunderbar!"); these e-mails root them, her and her husband, stake them in life, into the rich dirt of it. And the lovemaking grafts them to one another, commingles them, despite their having no children together, and besides, after ten years of doing it, it is a reliable pleasure. Eleven years. It is not as though they met yesterday, and are trying to figure out, will this work. He is a permanent part of her, of her life.

But it is the daily familiarity with her husband's body she is missing, the handling of his old knobby flesh. Aged flesh is so fertile, grows excrescences: papules, papillomas, skin tags, moles that have to be checked yearly; yet the hair thins out, underarm and pubic, as if the soil had changed to one that no longer supports that verdant shrubbery, but instead nourishes an astonishing variety of wild mushrooms—beautiful, if you have an eye. It is the feeling every part of him she misses, she has the longing to swallow him up, to own him, it is like owning one's babies. The baby is first of all a body, a mouth really. She loved feeding her babies. She'd squirt milk from her breasts halfway across the room in a great creamy arc, her husband running happily to intercept it with open mouth, get it in his hair, even one time in his eye, their three-year-old daughter standing by awed. Showing off, she was. *Fanfarronear*: to brag. And she loved carrying those babies . . . outside, inside, especially carrying them inside. Walking down a street, you were never alone—you had a secret, even when you were showing, the turnings, somersaults, flutter kicks. Even the giving birth was a secret. Oh, the husband was there and the obstetrician—but it was between her and the baby, all twisted together pushing and retreating and banging and molding and tearing and then the thrusting out, the astonishing bloody bursting forth! And she is handed over, all hers, the little girl's body with her sweet lips, and she is able to examine every part of her, she is not really separate, they aren't separate until years later when those girls wrench themselves away . . . pushing and retreating and banging and tearing all over again, only over years instead of hours. Have to, they had to, to live their own lives, although she felt a terrible sadness that they had to. Over . . . gone, those lovely girls . . .

What was over? What was gone? The girls weren't really gone, gone, gone, vide "Sara takes a bath with Sherbert the labradoodle." Whence the sadness? "Vacation"—was it from the same root as "vacate," "vacant"? She feels so empty.

A vacant apartment is what she feels like: after "deporta-
tion" of its Jewish occupants. Looted. By the shamefaced
neighbors. Or the grinning neighbors.

Why has she brought him here? Why have they come?
　　Cradle of culture, Mozart, Bach, Beethoven, Dürer,
Goethe . . .
　　Let bygones be bygones.
　　Why has she dragged them here, of all places, here, into the
heart of darkness? Has she some need to see in the dark? Some
need to see what was best not seen? Were there things that
were best not seen?
　　Nothing human is alien to me.
　　Really?

"You know, if you're really getting up three, four times a night
to pee—" She is practically yelling to be heard over the machine.
Suddenly she is worried that it is only the machine she is
hearing. Is his chest moving? Is he breathing? She elbows him,
and he groans, and she is grateful. "That's what you said, you
just told me that—three, four times a night—well, maybe you
ought to see Dr. Bela. You could have cancer or something."
　　"Huh?"
　　"Cancer. Maybe you have cancer."
　　"What are you talking about? It's the middle of the night!"
He does not remove the clear-plastic mask from his face,
although he knows his words are muffled. He expects to return
to sleep.
　　"Well," she laughs a little. "Cancer doesn't stop in the middle
of the night. Better call Dr. Bela when we get back."

"Cancer? Cancer from what? From not washing my hands? Let me sleep, will you." But he feels more awake now, unfortunately.

"From peeing. I mean, because you pee so much. That could be a sign of—some kind of—male cancer."

"Male cancer? What? What?"

"You sound like you're underwater. You know how you say 'women's cancer' or 'female problems' instead of calling it uterine cancer or ovarian cancer, you call it one of those cancers 'in there.'"

She points to where she imagines his genitals are, although she knows that even if his eyes are open, he cannot see these gestures of hers. She has the impulse to give his penis an affectionate pat, or maybe a nudge (or a light slap? odd thought), his sleeping penis. "Well," she goes on, "you have an 'in there,' too, not just an 'out there,' and you have lots of things 'out there' and 'in there.' Vulnerable things. Like the prostate. It's about the size of a kiwi fruit. Frequent peeing can be a sign of prostate cancer. Or difficulty peeing. Your PSA is okay. I don't think you can have prostate cancer without an elevated PSA, but I could be wrong.

"Or you could have testicular cancer, though peeing wouldn't have anything to do with that. You'd feel lumps and bumps." It's been weeks, probably more than two, since she's felt his balls, held that saggy bag of fruit in her hand, taken him in her mouth. She feels that dull ache again, low down in her.

It is not even that he can come very often that way, from her sucking him, he usually can't. Has some inhibition she doesn't understand, although she has asked him about it. Does he worry about making a mess in her mouth, dirtying her?

Maybe he thinks the taste is offensive to her, despite her reas-
surances that it is just a little sour, and half-sour pickles are a
favorite of hers. He doesn't talk enough, this husband; in many
ways, for all she knows him, she doesn't know him; he doesn't
know himself, doesn't need to know, he just *does* things, some
of them admirable. Goes about his business. Anyway, she has
reassured him and reassured him, but what gets through? Her
first husband loved it, although the sounds he made coming
are fading a little from her memory. Again she feels a sadness
start in her, and she doesn't resist it, although she tells herself,
well, at least he died a natural death with his family all around
him in the apartment, way he wanted. (Lung cancer, though
he never smoked a cigarette.) Tombstone (perpetual care).
Yearly pediatrics forum in his memory at NYU.

"Or you could have something common, like diabetes.
Although Bela checks for that. With all that peeing. Common.
But serious."

He twists the mask to the side so his mouth is free. "Why
are you doing a medical workup in the middle of the night?
Or at the crack of dawn, it's probably dawn by now. We're
on vacation! I've been getting up a bunch of times all my
life. Since my thirties. The same as now. You're just usually
asleep. I have a small bladder. You know that. You had me
get it tested years ago. It's small compared to the average man's.
Go to sleep. Let's just go back to sleep."

"I *can't*. You woke me up. I'd like some company, I
don't want to lie here by myself. I'd hold your hand if you'd
washed it."

"I'm not getting up to wash my hands. Take a pill if you
can't sleep."

"That's a nice husband." She shakes her head. "It's too close to morning to take a pill. I'll be hungover."

"Then read a book or something. You brought a ton of books. We paid overweight for them at the airport, we'll pay overweight on the trip back. Every one of those books will cost fifty bucks by the time we get home, and they're all paperbacks. Get a Kindle, use my iPad, you're Neanderthal woman lugging those books around."

"*I* paid for those books, *I* pay for my own overweight. What's it got to do with you?"

"What do you need all those *grim* books for?"

The Kindly Ones, The Third Reich at War, Slaughterhouse-Five, On the Natural History of Destruction. All of them about World War II. Maybe she'll find something in them, she doesn't know what.

Not touching him, she is lying next to him flat on her back, unmoving, although she has no expectation of sleep. She is keeping away from him. Why? She is keeping him up. Why? "History's a cesspool we drown in," she says.

"Where'd you get that?"

"I don't know." She raises her shoulders questioningly. "Read it somewhere. Seemed apt."

Now he wriggles out of the mask and lets it fall overboard, overbed, that is, what's the point, she has murdered sleep, although the machine keeps heaving out air. The *whishing* sound is there in the background as if someone is vacuuming.

She goes on: "What do you mean, 'It interrupts the flow'? That's what you said, right? You said you don't wash your hands in the middle of the night because it interrupts the flow. Are you stopping and starting? I mean, the urine, the stream?"

"No, no," he tells her. "It's like Niagara Falls. Fine, unfettered, and free is my pee. No, getting up a bunch of times during the night I try to maintain a certain rhythm, like I'm dancing, like I'm doing laps at the Columbia pool: I flow out of bed, do my thing, and flow back. Washing my hands would stop the flow."

"But you swore—"

"I doubt I said I'd do it during the night. Look, I wash my hands enough for a normal person. Most people *say* they wash their hands, but if monitors stand in public bathrooms, unobtrusively, they find that a small percentage of people actually do. I read an article that in Minnesota maybe thirty-three or thirty-four percent of people actually wash their hands."

"I didn't marry a Minnesotan. You promised! I should have put it in the prenup."

He laughs.

She doesn't. "You think I like toilet training an old geezer? I wash my hands twenty times a day."

"'It's your *job*. I don't work for the Health and Hospitals Corporation. You talk like the hand-washing police. I should make you a badge . . ." He sits up in the dark bed. "Look, it goes against my grain to do something senseless. I'm a rational being. I'm a scientist."

"A rational being? A scientist? Maybe you know about quarks and neutrinos but when it comes to germs, you don't know shit from Shinola."

She turns on the light at the bed table. She can see his large body; he is sitting up, and she suddenly feels he is obese and filthy. What is she doing with this man?

"Turn that off!" he yells.

"We're both up! Nobody's going to sleep anymore tonight!"

"Says who? Since when are you in charge here? Where's your whip?"

She looks around the room, dimly lit now by her bedside lamp. There is a print of bright yellow chrysanthemums above the desk. On the wall behind her—she twists her neck, hears that rustling sound again, turns her whole body—there is a print of geraniums, red in a clay pot. They're pleasant, sort of. And very red. She is in a cabin, on vacation. With her husband. Whom she loves.

"I wash my hands," he says tight teethed, "when they feel dirty, that's when I wash them."

"When they *feel* dirty? What kind of scientist are you?"

"Physics starts with feelings. With intuition—"

"But it doesn't stop there! You develop a theory, you test it. You, of all people, to go by *feelings!* You don't even know when you've left streaks of shit on the toilet seat. You leave shit in your underpants for Pearl to clean up! You're losing sphincter control. It happens as you get old. The gastroenterologist told you to do Kegel exercises. Do you do them? Un-uh."

"The maid's *supposed* to clean. That's her job!"

"Not your shit! Clean your own shit! It's the twenty-first century." She feels a jolt! Has he Tasered her? The cabin, the whole ship, recoils. "What's going on?" She cowers against the pillow.

"It's a lock." He laughs. "We're going through a lock. Canals. They're all over Germany. There are a hundred twenty-two locks. I told you that. We're going through eight of them tonight. You just don't know anything about terrain."

She straightens up. Waits through the ship's jumping several times more. Tries to get the shake out of her voice. "You disgust me!"

"Really? Shouldn't you consult with someone about that? Maybe the psychiatrist you want me to see? Because all I touch during the night is my dick and the doorknob. Only you touch my dick—well, not lately—and only you and the maid touch the doorknob. She wears gloves. And you, of course, are immaculate."

"I am *not* immaculate. You know that box of latex gloves I pack in my suitcase? They're not just for sex. I disimpact myself with them. I pull the shit out of me when the Metamucil doesn't work. And sometimes even when it does! I can't stand the feeling of bits of crap left behind. Little pellets, soft smooth globules . . ."

"Why do you have to tell me this? You think it's a turn-on?"

"Because it's true. You're so squeamish. We can't try anal intercourse because you think I'm filled with shit to the brim. You have no sense of anatomy. I can take an enema! You can use a condom! We can't lick each others' asses although I've got dental dams in the house. 'Nothing human is alien to me.' You ever heard of that? No, you're not a doctor."

"'Nothing human is alien to you.' Except for me! You ever hear of privacy, gentleness, respect for the soul?"

"Soul? *Schmole!* Since when do physicists talk about the soul! I should have married another doctor. Someone who's not afraid of shit. Who believes in the germ theory."

"Like your late sainted husband, I suppose. Did he bathe in Clorox?"

"Don't you even *mention* my husband! Your wife was a fat

pig, you were married to an aggressive fat pig. People tell me she walked all over you, blasted you in public."

"What? Who said that? People are prejudiced against women who speak their mind! You know that! And against women who are overweight! She had a very low metabolism. If she ate nothing, she gained weight. Anyway, I like a little cushion. When I lie on top of you, I feel like Brer Rabbit done landed in the briar patch."

"Well, keep out of my briar patch! Go find yourself another blubber patch!" She tries to lower her voice. "Brer Rabbit! You're more like a giant shmoo! Bela told you to take off ten pounds. Did you do it? Nah. You know more than Bela. Didn't your father have heart disease?"

"Healthy as an ox—"

"What did he die of? Health?"

"Kidney failure . . ."

"Secondary to what?"

"What do you mean?"

"Oh come on . . . caused by what?"

"They said high blood pressure."

"Well, high blood pressure leads to heart disease. And it also blows out your kidneys. He snored, didn't he?"

He reluctantly nods.

"You told me you have a *mild* case of sleep apnea and you only have to use the machine when you feel like it. You have a *severe* case! You stop breathing sixty times an hour! You're even Cheyne-Stoking when you sleep! Your brain doesn't talk to your lungs! Dying people do Cheyne-Stokes breathing! You need to use that goddamn machine every minute. Use it when you're awake!"

"Tell me, tell me." With his hands, he beckons her to him belligerently. "Nag away! Your daughter says you're the worst nag outside of a barn."

"I can imagine which daughter. So dear of you to repeat that! Real emotional intelligence! Weren't you valedictorian— of your high school class? A straight-A idiot! You don't know anything, except maybe outer space. You don't even know that you're going to die!"

"Of course, I'll die! Everyone dies! You're going to die, too!"

"And the worst of it is, you might not get the big bang, Mr. Einstein. You could have a series of small bangs—one stroke and then another and another—tiny, tiny, hardly detectable; and you won't be Mr. Know-it-all anymore! Or you could have multiple, minuscule infarcts slowly, over time. To your heart. Silent infarcts. You could be having one right now! And then you won't be moving around very much, let alone playing tennis. You'll be in bed, on oxygen. And you don't have adequate long-term nursing care because you never thought to buy it when you were in good enough health to qualify. You figure I want to hang around the apartment taking care of you twenty-four seven? Why don't you just drop dead already, like right now?"

At six forty-five, they sit at breakfast, the first people in the dining hall, sunlight pouring through the portholes onto the rows and rows of unoccupied tables. Tables covered with starched white cloths laid with shiny silver-plated flatware, fresh yellow daisy centerpieces—the whole place is ablaze. He eats his granola, sips his caffe latte with three sugars and reads

intensely an article in the *Scientific American* he has brought
from home—a piece about fracking practices around the
world. Some German music is coming over the loudspeaker,
but he blocks it out. Tries to concentrate on fracking: fractur-
ing the earth's surface, polluting the water supply with chemicals, causing earthquakes.

Old newspaper pieces from back pages of the *New York
Times* are bobbling around in his head, interfering with his
reading. Annoying.

Indian from India hires hitmen to kill wife, he is out walking
with her on a Sunday in some park in Queens, hitmen shoot
him, too, in the leg so he looks innocent.

Naked man masturbating on roof of building, throws bricks
down at women passersby below—Williamsburg section of
Brooklyn. Kills a woman before police get to him.

Why do they put crap like that in a fine paper like the *New
York Times*? You'd think it was the *Enquirer*.

Why can't he get this rot out of his mind? Fracking,
fracking . . .

She doesn't attend much to the music either—a requiem? An
oratorio or opera, something big and Germanic and over-
whelming with a chorus and an orchestra. And there is something terribly, irredeemably wrong with the recording, the
speed is off, she doesn't know what exactly, she tries not to
listen, wouldn't mind going deaf. In (graduated) prescription
sunglasses, she sits at the table and chews without appetite the
dwarf neutered bagels (*bobes tam*) with smoked salmon, onions,
capers (hold the cream cheese), drinks black coffee, and reads
and rereads the first paragraph of *If This Is a Man* while she

tries not to remember what she said to him (did she really say . . .), what he said to her, and tries not to hear what she is trying not to say to herself: that she will never ever again shoot milk across a room for anyone, let alone for that slender wiry fellow with the thick head of bright brown hair who'd run for it mouth open as if it were manna; never ever hear again or even remember the sounds he made coming in her mouth or in her cunt or in her ass, the dear, dear sounds, never ever even hear him say again, "I've got the easy part, I'm dying." That she would soon enough have the easy part, too, and she would spend the greater part of the time before that, that brief blink of an eye before the final blackness, with this blind, doughy, kindly man who couldn't latch on.

They did not make love until they got to Luxembourg.

ACKNOWLEDGMENTS

THE PERSON WHO is most responsible for *Scary Old Sex* coming out of the dark is Sandra Newman. She edited these stories with patience, respect, a few tears and belly laughs, without any prudishness, and always with the highest literary intelligence. And she introduced me to her agent, Victoria Hobbs, who knows publishers' sensibilities so well that she managed to get three offers within a month on this first book, a collection of short stories by an unknown author—a miracle akin to Moses parting the Red Sea.

Alexandra Pringle, editor-in-chief, fell in love with *Scary Old Sex* and presented it winningly to Bloomsbury on both sides of the ocean; I am grateful. And Kathy Belden, my in-house editor, gently and respectfully suggested cuts and commas, and tried to keep me reality-bound: e.g., lilacs do not bloom in New York in July.

Judith Viorst, my friend for more than thirty years, read each of these stories in many different versions, some of them novel length, and shored up my confidence in myself as writer and person.

Ruth Ahntholz (pen name Ruth Lilian) has also read and

reread these stories, besides novels and stories that didn't make it into this collection, that didn't make it anywhere; and she sat with me in writers' groups and through dark nights.

Barry Malzberg's hyperbolic appreciation of me as a writer has cheered me on since I was twenty-two.

Jo Anne Simson, friend of fifty years and polymath, taught me the science I needed to know to write "Artifact."

Lisa Vergara, art historian, enabled me to write more confidently about the art world in the story "In Love with Murray"; and she proofread each story for me with precision and thoughtfulness.

Otto Kernberg and Jerome Levine helped in immeasurable ways.

Bernard Malamud was a climate to me—his jokes, his Jewish atheism, his aliveness, his loving-kindness, his feeling for art and for me, his total immersion in literature, and, above all, his writing.

A NOTE ON THE AUTHOR

ARLENE HEYMAN earned a B.A. at Bennington College, an M.F.A. from Syracuse University, and her M.D. from the University of Pennsylvania. She is the recipient of Woodrow Wilson, Fulbright, Rockefeller, and Robert Wood Johnson fellowships. Heyman has been published in *New American Review*, won *Epoch* magazine's novella contest for an earlier version of "Artifact," and has been listed twice in the honor rolls of *The Best American Short Stories*. Heyman is a psychiatrist/psychoanalyst practicing on the Upper West Side of Manhattan, where she lives with her husband. She is currently at work on a novel.